ONE NIGHT SERIES

DANA ISALY

GAMES WE PLAY

Published: Dana Isaly 2021

Editing: Sandra at One Love Editing
Cover Design: Pink Elephant Designs
Formatting: Pink Elephant Designs

THEME SONG

Dazed and Confused by Ruel

WARNING

This book is strictly for those over the age of legal adulthood. It contains graphic sexual content. There is material in this novella that some may find triggering. There is dark subject matter including violence, eating disorders, a lot of bad words, and BDSM themes. The content in this book is a work of fiction and fantasy. It is not meant to depict realistic BDSM activities. There is a scene that describes attempted suicide.

If you or anyone you know is in emotional distress or experiencing suicidal thoughts, please know there is help. Call the National Suicide Prevention Lifeline at 800-273-8255. The National Suicide Prevention Lifeline is a United States-based suicide prevention network of over 160 crisis centers that provides 24/7 service via a toll-free hotline. (Available in English and Spanish)

Alternate numbers for these countries:

Canada: 833-456-4566

United Kingdom: 116 123

Australia: 13 11 14

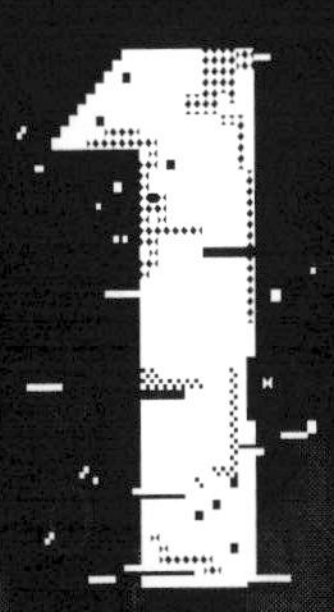

The doorbell rang, and I groaned outwardly, probably loud enough for her to hear through the door. The only reason I knew the interviewer was a woman was because my lawyer had brought the papers by to show me she had signed all of the NDAs, her loopy scrawl painted across each page.

It wasn't really my choice to sit down for an interview, and I really hoped as I made my way to my front door that this wouldn't take longer than an hour. Hopefully she had done her homework on me, and I could get her in and out and go back to hiding away.

I tugged my hoodie over my head and pulled it down across my forehead as much as I could. The mask I wore for streaming had a wild, manic-looking smile on it, and I pulled that up over the bridge of my nose.

I opened my door to a pretty face surrounded by a halo of dark auburn waves. She smiled up at me with a mouth full of straight white teeth. I saw the small scar on her bottom lip that looked like it was from an old piercing. Dressed the way she was in her tight slacks and buttoned blazer, I would've never pegged her for the type to have piercings.

She was a good foot shorter than me, which caused her to have to crane her neck back to look at me, giving me a glimpse straight down into her ample cleavage. My dick twitched.

Fuck, she's gorgeous.

"Oh, hi!" She reached out her hand as she took in my covered face. "I'm Quinlan. You can call me Quin." I reached out and took the slender little thing in my own. "I signed the NDAs. You don't have to wear the mask." She pulled her hand back, and I stepped to the side to let her in. Even through the mask, I could smell her sweet perfume.

"I have trust issues," I said with a wink. She gave me a shy smile and walked the rest of the way in, looking around my open-plan apartment. I shut the door and ushered her into the kitchen. She hopped up on one of the barstools and pulled her laptop out of her messenger bag, instantly making herself at home.

"Do you want a drink?"

Her big brown eyes swiveled to me, and she blinked before a blush crept over her cheeks. "I...I can't. I'm working."

"I meant water or something, Quinlan," I said with a soft laugh. The blush turned into a bright red stain, blotchy and too fucking cute. I wondered what other parts of her would look like lit up like that.

"Oh, no, I'm fine. Thank you." She cleared her throat, opened her laptop, and pulled out her recorder. "Did you just wake up?"

I leaned my hip against the counter and looked down at her. "About thirty minutes ago. Why?"

"You sound like you're still half-asleep." Her smile was soft and teasing.

"This is just my voice, love." Had she not done any research on me? "I'm primarily known for my voice. Didn't you do your homework?"

She shook her head, typing away on her laptop and getting everything set up. "I like to try and go in as blind as possible. I feel like it helps me ask better questions. More authentic."

I groaned inwardly. That meant it wasn't going

to be a quick in-and-out type of interview. This was going to take a while.

She paused and looked up. "I don't know a thing about you, Joker. Does that wound your ego?"

Yes, I thought instantly. I wanted her to know about me, be impressed by what I'd built for myself. Why did it bother me so much that she didn't know who I was?

"Come on, then," I said, walking around the counter to where she was sitting. "Let me show you what I do for a living before you start asking questions. Give you a glimpse into my world."

"Okay," she drawled. "But I've seen plenty of gaming setups. It's kind of my job." She jumped down, and I had to force myself to ignore the way her tits bounced underneath that blazer. I wanted her to take it off. I wanted to see the smooth skin of her shoulders and slender arms.

I mentally shook myself when I realized she was just staring at me, waiting for me to lead the way. I took off toward the back of my home where my gaming room was.

"It's your job, but you don't know anything about the people you go to interview?" I flicked a switch as I entered, lighting the entire room up in blue LEDs. She stood in the doorway watching me as I made my way over to my computer and started pushing buttons and getting everything turned on and lit up.

"I know *of* you. I just don't know a whole lot about you. I like to learn as the people learn." She smiled and looked around the room, taking everything in.

"So this is where the magic happens," I said, gesturing to the desk that was now backlit in a bright green.

She took a few steps in and made her way around the room, looking at all of my posters and running her fingers over my shelves that held all of my manga. I crossed my arms over my chest and leaned against the wall to watch her.

"That's an impressive collection," she said before moving around the room and stopping at my desk. She plopped her short frame right into my chair and did a spin. "Comfy."

"I spend a lot of time in it. It needs to be."

"Does every surface in here light up? What is it with gamers and LEDs?" She laughed, and I found I liked the way her face lit up.

"Not every surface," I said. "But when I stream, I don't like any bright lights. It's easier to keep my face hidden if it's a bit darker in here."

She nodded and took another look around. "It's nice. Why don't we do the interview in here? It'll be more in your element. Help you not be so nervous."

"I'm not nervous."

"Stop fidgeting, then," she said with a grin. And then she was out of the room to go grab her things. When she came back, I was sitting in my computer chair, and she took up residence on the couch across from me. She shrugged out of her blazer, exposing the brightly colored tattoos covering every inch of her arms and shoulders.

"Sleeves?" I asked. "I never would've expected that."

That slight blush crawled across her cheeks again. The little scar on her lip made more sense now.

"I try to dress professionally. It doesn't mean I'm a prude. Do you have any tattoos?"

I was dressed in jeans and a long-sleeved hoodie. Not an inch of skin was showing on me besides my hands, a bit of my neck, and my eyes. So she couldn't see that I was actually covered in them.

"Off the record?"

"Sure," she chirped.

"I do. I just don't really tell anyone about them for the whole identity thing. I've got my left arm done and a few on my chest. My legs are almost completely covered."

"I have my hip tattooed, like my upper thigh and up onto my hip bone, and holy shit that hurt. Leg pain is a whole different type of pain."

My eyes grazed across her body and settled on her hip for a moment, wondering what kind of tattoo she had there. She cleared her throat, and I looked back up at her, our eyes meeting for a moment longer than seemed professional. The air between us felt heavy and charged. I watched her slender neck move as she swallowed nervously.

"What questions do you have for me, Quinlan?" I asked to break the silence that had stretched on too long. I would have loved to sit there and watch her squirm under my gaze, but I figured with this being a professional meeting and not a personal one, I shouldn't make her too uncomfortable.

But I couldn't stop thinking about her arms and legs tied to the bed, her body open and waiting for me. Or maybe her on her hands and knees, a collar around that pretty petite neck, following me around like a good little girl. Her mouth wrapped around my cock. That ass painted red from my toys.

"Let's start at the beginning," she said, startling me out of my daydream. I crossed my legs and pulled my hoodie down a bit, hoping to hide my growing erection. "What got you into all of this?"

She pulled her feet up under herself and settled in. Her wide brown eyes settled on mine, and I wondered if she could see that one was blue and one was brown. It was probably my biggest insecurity. And, of course, it was normally the first thing anyone noticed about me and couldn't help but comment on. But she hadn't said a word.

"Money," I stated bluntly. She gave a small laugh. I leaned back in my chair and got comfortable, trying to get the blood pumping to my brain instead. "I always enjoyed gaming, and once I realized I could make money off of it, I decided I might as well try streaming. I got better and better at it. More people were joining every time I played. I honestly think a lot of people started joining mainly to listen to me talk and not because I was actually good at what I was doing."

"And you were okay with that?"

"Sure," I said and shrugged. "Money is money. If they want to sit there and listen to me talk, who am I to stop them?"

"Do you get requests? Like do people ask you to say certain things or say hi to them?" She chewed on her lip as she asked the question and typed a few notes on her laptop. I stared at it as I answered.

"Yes. All the time. And a lot of the time it's sexual." Her eyes went wide, and she stopped typing. That adorable fucking blush crept up her neck again, and I smiled under my mask. I loved that I was the cause behind that.

"Sexual?" she asked as she pulled her eyes from her screen to me.

"Oh yeah, Curly Q," I said, leaning forward and propping my elbows on my knees. "You'd be surprised with the things people have paid me to say to them." I watched her swallow again, my mind straying to something else she could swallow. And when her next question came out breathy and strained, I knew it was over. She was about to be a fly caught in my web.

"What kind of things?"

I grinned.

"A lot of people have certain kinks they like me to play into. Have you ever heard of having a degradation or a praise kink, Quinlan?"

That blush crawled from her neck up over her cheeks as she tried to laugh it off.

"I've heard of it, yes. Can't say I've ever experienced it. I would never kink shame anyone, but I don't really understand the whole degradation thing. I'm not sure why anyone would want to be humiliated like that."

"There's a lot of reasons. For some people, it's a release. They get to let go in the bedroom and let someone else be in charge. The taboo aspect of it is a big turn-on for a lot of people, too." If she didn't stop chewing on that bottom lip… I took a deep breath. "Anyway, they will ask me to say little phrases, and they send me tokens and shit for it, which is just a fancy way of paying me."

"So you get money to sit there and stream and win competitions, but you also play into people's fantasies about you?"

"I don't know if I would say that they are fantasies about me specifically, but yes."

"Oh, I'm sure they are. People have this fascination with internet personalities. Especially people like you who have this whole sexy mystery about them. With your deep voice and mask you're constantly wearing—brings out the mask kink in all of us."

"All of us?" I asked, leaning back in my chair and giving her a smirk from under my mask. "Does that include yourself, Quinlan? Do you have a thing for masks?" I tilted my head to the side and let my gaze slide along her body before returning to her face. She met my gaze and didn't waver, even though I saw her chest rise and fall a bit quicker. To know that I incited that reaction from her made the blood rush right to my dick.

I had to fight back a groan. I wanted to cross the

space between us and show her my dark side, show her everything I could make her feel. I wanted to show her that if she could trust me for a night, I would make her feel everything she was afraid to feel. She moved her legs and rubbed her thighs together subtly. Was she turned on? Maybe I wasn't the only one feeling the stupid amount of electrical charge between us. She cleared her throat.

"I thought I was the one that was supposed to be asking the questions?" She was trying to change the subject. I stood up and walked over to her, scooting a few of her things out of the way and sitting opposite her.

"Yes, Quinlan. Go ahead. Ask the questions." I purposefully lowered my voice an octave just to throw her a bit more off-balance.

This interview had quickly turned into something far more dangerous, but I wasn't about to fight it. There was something about her that drew me in. I wanted to see her crawl across the floor for me. I wanted to strip her bare, tie her up in pretty knots, and tease her within an inch of her life. I leaned back against the couch and turned my gaze on her.

"What about your childhood, Joker? Is that off-limits?" She smirked at me, and I found myself smiling back. I was disappointed she hadn't taken that bait, but it was still early.

"Not all of it," I answered.

"Okay, then. Let's start from the very beginning. Were you always a nerd?" She looked over at me, and her smile was all flirt.

"A nerd? You interview people like me for a living. Do you insult all of the people you interview, Curly Q? Or just the ones you find attractive?"

She threw her head back and laughed, hitting my arm lightly and exposing the creamy column of her throat. She looked back at me.

"Bold of you to assume I find you attractive. How would I? I've only managed to see your eyes."

"They're nice eyes though, no?"

She paused and looked at me. "They are." We stared at each other for a moment, just looking at each other. I wondered if she could feel the gravitational pull that seemed to be holding us together, begging us to touch. "Get on with it, then. When did this obsession with gaming and computer stuff begin?"

"When I was really young, I think I would've had an interest in it, but we were just too poor to afford anything I would need to get into it. Once I was in high school, I was able to get a job after classes and on weekends. I saved a lot and then started spending a lot. I managed to get quite the setup. Once I started to get everything I needed, I was able to really focus on playing."

"So instead of spending your high school years out with girls, you decided to stay up all night playing games. And you wouldn't call yourself a nerd?" she teased.

"Trust me, if girls were interested back then, I would've been out with them instead."

"I find that hard to believe. Girls not interested in you?" Her eyebrows knitted together as she typed a few notes into her laptop.

"A tall noodle boy that didn't know how to dress or speak in coherent sentences around girls? I wasn't that much of a catch, darling. It wasn't until I was in college that I started to fill out and care about taking care of myself. Not that I'm a bodybuilder, but I put some muscle on, started caring what I looked like..." I trailed off.

She chewed on her bottom lip while she typed away on her keyboard. "And you went to college for?" she asked, looking up at me from under her long lashes.

"Computer Science."

"Shocker."

"My life kind of took a turn in college. The confidence I had found outside of the bedroom started translating into confidence inside the bedroom. I started to get a reputation for a certain type of...experience when it came to sex."

She tried to hide a smile, but I saw the small twitch of her mouth before she recovered. If I didn't know any better, I would have thought she was interested in what exactly I had meant.

"And that led to the whole..." She paused, and I could see her trying to find the right words for what she was trying to get at. "That led to the whole saying sexy things for people online gig?"

"Eventually," I answered. "I started to notice girls I was talking to reacting a certain way to my voice and to the things I would say. So when I got out of college, I started streaming full-time and thought I would test the waters for that kind of shit. And it worked. So I figured I might as well get paid for it."

"Yeah, but now you have to hide away all the time. Doesn't that get lonely?" Her question caught me off guard, and I had to think a moment before answering. Had I been lonely?

"There are so many people that aren't part of this world I'm in," I told her while thinking out loud. "I can normally go out, and no one will know me. No one knows what I look like, and it would take someone that was really well acquainted with my streams to recognize my voice. A lot of guys have deep voices. And I have to get groceries somehow."

She laughed at my little joke and then tilted her head as she looked me up and down. "Tell me some of the things people have asked for," she blurted. I blinked. That seemed to have come out of nowhere. She looked up at me with a little spark in her eyes that threw down a challenge.

Would I actually show her this side of me?

The answer was yes. *Fuck* yes.

My little pet did want to play, after all.

"This has to be off the record, Quinlan. I don't want people thinking I took advantage of you, and I don't want you to take this and twist my words to make it seem like I said these things to you inappropriately."

She took a deep breath, seemingly steadying herself, and closed her laptop with a satisfying click. She made sure everything else was turned off and sat it all on the floor at our feet.

She turned back to me, crossing her legs like a pretzel underneath her. I put my arm on the back of the couch and reached out, running my fingers through her hair. Fuck, it was soft.

"Better?" she asked, her voice shaking slightly.

I nodded.

"Do you want to play a game with me, Quinlan?"

She looked unsure of herself but took a deep breath.

"Yes."

I smiled.

"Are you going to be a good girl for me tonight, Quinlan?"

Her eyes widened, but she didn't answer. She didn't realize that this was where the night was going to take a turn. It was my turn to take over this little interview and turn it into something far more fun for the both of us.

"I asked you a question," I stated. "It would be in your best interest to answer. I don't like repeating myself." I took a firmer hold on her hair, just tight enough that she would feel it start to pull at her scalp. "I'll ask one...more...time." My voice dropped even lower, and I saw her throat move as she swallowed. "Are you going to be a good girl for me tonight?"

She nodded, eyes wide and trained on me.

"Yes, sir is the appropriate answer."

She took a small breath through her parted lips, and then on a sigh, the sweetest sound came from her mouth.

"Yes, sir."

My entire body was liquid heat at hearing those words. I looked over at her and let my eyes wander across every inch of her body, praying that she was feeling the same way I was.

How far is she going to let me take this?

Her full lips were still parted. Her chest was panting quickly in and out. I could see through her thin tank that her nipples were hardening. I barely bit back a groan thinking about them in my mouth.

I gathered more of her hair in my fist and pulled her head back, exposing more of her neck. I leaned closer, our knees touching and my face hovering over hers. Her pupils were blown wide with lust. And just as I was about to speak, she did something that made every ounce of blood in my body rush painfully to my dick.

She smiled. It was a smile that made me want to smack it off her pretty face.

She laughed a throaty laugh that was all sex.

"Seems like you're doing more than just telling me some phrases, Joker."

"My name is Jack."

Her grin grew wider. "I know," she said.

Oh, yeah, I thought. *The NDAs.*

"Are you going to take off that mask or..." She trailed off as she reached up to pull my mask off my face. My other hand wrapped around her wrist before she could touch the fabric, and I not so gently placed her hand back on her lap. I shook my head back and forth. She stuck her bottom lip out in a pout. *Brat.* I abandoned her hand to run my thumb across that bottom lip.

"You have the real thing here in front of you instead of through a computer screen. Might as well get the full effect. What do you think, Quinlan?"

"You may as well be behind the computer screen. I can't see you. Let me see you."

My hand slipped from her mouth to her jaw and down around her throat. I squeezed enough to make my point.

"Now, now, Quinlan, love." I raised up on my knees to hover farther above her. Her head craned back to look up at me. She bit her lip and leaned into my hand that was still wrapped around her throat. "You don't get to make demands. You get to sit down, shut up, and do as you're told."

"I—"

I cut her off before she could say anything by squeezing even harder on the sides of her neck.

"No, Quinlan. This is how this is going to go." I took a breath. I could do it. I could convince her to let me do everything I was dreaming up in my head.

"You're going to give me your consent to do this. One night with me, Q," I continued. "You're going to choose a safe word. And then I am going to use your body in every way imaginable. I am going to take my time with you. I am going to own it. I am going to push you past your limits. And you will beg me for more. I'm going to punish that tight little cunt of yours until you can't think of anything else but me. Do you understand?"

I followed the bob of her throat as she swallowed.

"Yes, sir."

I breathed a sigh of relief. *Holy shit.* She wanted it. She had agreed.

"That's my good girl," I murmured, and she lit up under that small amount of praise like a flower to the sun. I held her face in my hands to keep her gaze on me.

"Give me your consent, Quinlan." By that point, I had worked myself up so much for it, I was prepared to beg her. I would have gotten down on my knees for her. I needed her to let me worship her body the only way I knew how.

She took a deep breath and closed her eyes, leaning toward my body. I threaded my hands through her hair and leaned down closer to her face, suddenly wishing I didn't have my mask on. But I couldn't take it off. Not yet. Her little comment about mask kinks didn't get past me. I had a feeling even though she wanted to see my face, she wanted this more.

"Yes," she breathed, opening her eyes and finding mine again. "I'm doing this." She sounded like she was still trying to convince herself. Not that I could really blame her. She had known me for all of forty-five minutes and I was already asking for her permission to fuck her senseless. That was so much of the appeal though. My body hummed with excitement. "One random night with a random guy who claims he can rock my world." She gave a small laugh.

There were so many things I wanted to do.

"You're doing this," I confirmed. "Safe words. Red means stop. If you say this at any time, I will immediately stop what I am doing. Yellow means slow down, you're approaching your limit. And green means go," I ended with a smile. "But you can trust that I will stop at any point in time you need me to."

"What are you going to do to me, Joker?" she breathed.

Her hands that had been motionless in her lap this entire time now moved to my waist where she curved her fingers through my belt loops. She gave me a little tug, and I let my body move a bit closer to her.

"First," I said as I dipped down, moving my nose along the side of her neck and up to her ear, taking in the scent of her even through my mask. Her head lolled to the side, and I saw gooseflesh break out across her skin. "I'm going to let you shower. I am going to shower. And then I'm going to give you a glimpse into my world. And you're going to realize how freeing it is to give in to things you never thought you'd like."

She shivered against me.

"Let go for a night, Q. Let me help you let go."

Those big brown eyes turned to me, and I grabbed her hand to lead her to the spare bathroom and set her up with everything she would need. She looked a little hesitant, but when I told her I would be on the other side of the house also taking a shower, she started stripping before I could even get out of the room.

"You're sure you don't want to just stay in here and join me?" I watched her top drop to the floor. My eyes roamed across her chest. Her breasts were fucking phenomenal. She was wearing a black lace bra, and I could just see the hint of her perfect pink nipples underneath.

Her fingers went to the button on her jeans, and she shimmied out of those as well. It took all the willpower I had to not drop to my knees and nip at the soft flesh of her tummy and hips. Those thighs moved against themselves as she stepped out of the jeans, leaving her in a matching set of lace panties.

"Get in the fucking shower," I growled. "And come find me when you're done." She smirked and reached behind her to unclasp her bra. I slammed the bathroom door shut so hard behind me as I left I was sure I cracked it.

This woman was going to be the death of me.

After my own shower, I threw on a white T-shirt, black boxer briefs, and some jeans. I sank into the couch that faced the hallway where the spare bath was located. I would see her the moment she opened the bathroom door.

I had left my hoodie off, wanting her to see a little more of me. My tattoos on my arm were now on full display, as was my hair. It might not seem like a lot to most people, but most people didn't have to worry about anyone recognizing them on the street. I still wore the mask across my nose and mouth.

When the door finally opened, it did so slowly. She stepped out only wrapped in a towel. When her eyes landed on me, she turned shy. Her eyes dropped to the floor, and her cheeks flamed.

"I wasn't sure if I was supposed to put my clothes back on."

"Look at me," I ordered from my perch on the couch. Her head snapped up, her eyes meeting mine immediately. Fuck, she was a good listener. "Drop the towel." She took a deep breath. I was going to give her to the count of ten in my head before I threatened her and asked again. I didn't even make it to three before she released her death grip and it puddled around her feet.

My cock was instantly pressing against the zipper of my jeans, begging to be released. My eyes scanned across the few tattoos she had on her calves and then the one that circled from the top of her thigh up onto her hip. Her pussy was smooth, and I could already see it glistening from here, ready for me.

Her hip dips, the soft curve of her belly, and pert breasts were just begging to be squeezed, licked, and sucked on. She had tattoos covering both of her arms, and they stretched across her chest and in between her breasts where they stopped. When my eyes finally found themselves back on her face, she was looking at her feet, trying to shield her face with her hair.

"Get on your hands and knees." Her eyebrows knitted together, but she did as I said. "Crawl to me."

"And if I don't?"

I smiled behind my mask.

"Then I get to punish you. And before you even think about being a little brat and pushing me to punish you because you think you'll enjoy it...you won't. I'll make you hurt, baby. Now fucking crawl to me like the dog you are."

4

Her hips swung back and forth as she made her way over to me. She made the wise decision to listen this time around. She wasn't in the right headspace yet to accept the type of punishment I would dole out.

"Sit."

She settled herself in between my legs as I leaned forward and took her chin in my hand to force her eyes up to mine. A bit of defiance shown in them, and I couldn't wait to fuck that right out of her.

I pressed two of my fingers on her lips, and she opened her mouth just enough for them to slip in. Her tongue slipped between my digits, and she closed her lips, sucking them farther into her hot wet mouth. I groaned and pushed them even farther, testing her patience and gag reflex.

Not that it mattered. I would be fucking her tight little throat tonight whether she could handle it or not. I hoped she couldn't. I wanted to see her lipstick smeared across her face and my dick, her tears and mascara rolling over her cheeks. Oh, God, the sounds she would make as I forced her to take me to the hilt.

The tips of my fingers reached the back of her mouth, and I pushed into her throat, testing the waters. She coughed and gagged, her eyes never leaving mine.

Perfect.

I rolled my fingers around in her mouth a few more times until I had them so wet some spit was rolling over her lips and down onto her chin.

"Good dog," I cooed. Her eyes lit up with a bit of anger, but she held my gaze and didn't move. "Tell me, Quinlan. Are you wet for me?" Her breathing picked up. "Is this doing it for you, pet?"

I leaned forward and tapped my fingers on her right thigh, telling her to open up. She shuffled and spread her legs a bit wider for me. My hand squeezed her thighs before my fingertips slowly and lightly trailed over her slit. I didn't even have to push any farther to feel the wetness gathering there. She was soaked.

"You're dripping, little pet." I looked up from my fingers and met her closed eyes and parted mouth. I grinned. "Eyes open," I said as I pushed the tip of my finger through her folds and against her swollen clit.

She gasped, and her eyes flew open as she gripped onto my knees to keep herself from falling. I made small circles around that little bundle of nerves but not quite touching it. Three circles, and then I slowly slipped my finger inside of her. I watched her face as her body became hot and flushed.

I sank to my knees in front of her, keeping up the same pattern. Three circles and then one finger inside of her. No more. Just one. Just enough to feel me.

"Don't take your eyes off of me, understood?" I asked.

"Yes, sir," she breathed. She wasn't going to be able to hold herself up much longer, so I slipped an arm around her as I kept up my slow, methodical assault on her clit. Her body felt amazing pressed up against my own. She kept her eyes on me even though they threatened to roll to the back of her head a few times.

"Do you want to come?" She whimpered and nodded her head. "Then beg me for it."

"Please," she mewled. "Please let me come. I'm begging you. I need it. Please."

I pressed her tighter against my body, grinding my dick against her belly. I wasn't sure how long I was going to be able to make it myself. I did not want to come in my jeans like an overly excited teenager. We were going to need to do something about it before I exploded.

"Of course you can, my sweet little slut. Come for me," I said. A pitiful whimper came out of her mouth that went straight to my cock or my ego, I didn't know which. Probably both. "Come." I pushed my finger inside of her, letting the heel of my hand push against her clit at the same time.

She broke.

She came apart on my hand, falling into my chest and gripping my T-shirt so hard I thought she'd rip it. She let out a moan that was more of a scream into my chest as her pussy clenched around my finger.

Once she had come down, her breaths

becoming more even, I pulled my finger from her cunt and brought it to her mouth.

"You made a mess. Better lick it clean."

She pushed away from my chest and met my stare. "You caused the mess. You clean it up," she said, crossing her arms over her chest.

I laughed, and before she could react, reached out and slapped her across the face with the hand she had just been riding. Not hard enough to leave a mark, but hard enough to make it sting. I gripped her face as it flew to the side and pulled her attention back to me.

Holy shit, she was pissed. If looks could light fires, I would have been incinerated on the spot. Fuck, she was hot like that. Still a bit sweaty from her orgasm, a faint pink handprint on her cheek, and fire in her eyes.

"Only good girls get orgasms, Q. Naughty sluts get punishment. Do you want orgasms, or do you want me to tie you to my bed and whip you until you can't breathe?"

She stared me down, clearly wanting to say more but knowing her mouth would get her in more trouble than she was willing to accept.

Her mouth opened, and I let go of her face to hold my finger in front of her face. I had been using my middle finger, so it brought me great joy to see her get even more angry when she realized I was flipping her off.

She did a pretty good job licking her cum off my finger and even took the time to make sure the others were clean. When she was satisfied with her work, she sat back on her heels and looked up at me, waiting for my next command. I stood up to make my way to the game room.

"Come on, pet."

She moved to stand up and follow me, but that wasn't what I meant.

"Ah, ah," I tsked.

She looked up at me. "What now?"

I adjusted my still-hard cock and crouched down in front of her.

"That mouth of yours is very pretty. But if you keep talking to me with all that sass, I will fuck your mouth until you're too sore to talk, okay?"

She smiled and leaned toward me, going on all fours and pushing her hips up to give me a good view of her ass.

"Yes, sir," she said sweetly and a bit sarcastically. She pressed closer until she was able to press the side of her face against mine. Her skin was so fucking soft. She took my ear between her teeth.

"You smell so good," she said as she kissed where my mask met my jaw. "I bet you taste just as good," she purred. Her tongue darted out and licked up the side of my neck.

She moved so that she could look at me. Once her brown eyes met mine, I reached up to stroke down her face and over the cheek I had slapped just moments ago. She smiled and leaned into my hand. Poor lamb. My hand closed around her throat, and I watched the smirk drop from her face.

"Did I say you could touch me, dog?" That determined scowl settled back into place, and I gave the sides of her neck a little extra squeeze to make my point before standing back up.

"You will be crawling when you follow me around this house until you've proven yourself worthy of being allowed to walk. Understood?"

She stared straight ahead. "Yes, sir."

"Good girl." I patted the top of her head. "Come on, then."

I had her sit next to the couch while I went in search of things to make a little dog bed for her. I grabbed a few pillows and a blanket off my bed and laid everything on the ground next to my computer desk. While I was in there, I grabbed a collar and leash from my stash of toys and brought them into the game room as well.

I sat down and called her over to me. The sight of her crawling on her hands and knees to me would never be something I would get used to. Her hips were so fucking perfect it made it hard for me to breathe. Her skin was flawless, with the cutest stretch marks dotting her hips and ass. I wanted to lick each and every one of them.

I fiddled with the buckle on the collar and got it

to fit around her neck, making sure I could still stick two fingers between it and her before attaching the leash. The moment it was clasped around her neck, her muscles relaxed.

Sometimes that happened. Some people needed a little something extra to make them relax, make them feel a little less naked and bared to the world. It was the same concept as people who enjoyed Shibari because it relaxed them, the pressure on their muscles holding them securely. I wondered if she would enjoy being tied up in pretty little knots as well.

She sat back on her heels and looked up at me, her eyes softer than they had been. I took a moment to look her over. I was still solid as a rock, but I wasn't going to let her touch me just yet. I wanted her to want it so badly she could barely stand it.

"I have to stream for a bit. Make yourself comfortable." I motioned to the makeshift dog bed I had made for her next to me. She smiled, and it didn't hold the same challenge as it had before. This one was soft and sweet.

When she had made herself comfortable, I tied the leash to my chair and set up for streaming. My thoughts were completely consumed by her. I had been with plenty of other women. Not enough to make it gross, but I had seen my fair share. And I had enjoyed controlling them, owning them for the night.

But none of them had taken me like she had. I could remember exactly what she had felt like as she came on my fingers, squeezing me. I couldn't stop thinking how amazing she was going to feel when I finally slid into her. I looked down at her out of the corner of my eye and watched her eyes flutter closed as she rested her head against my thigh.

Something pulled at my chest at the sight, and I pushed that way the fuck down before turning my attention back to getting everything set up. Playing with the lights, I got everything set up the way I wanted. Trying not to move her too much, I leaned over and grabbed the hoodie that I normally wore off my desk.

I shrugged it on, pulled the hood up, and made sure my mask was still covering the lower half of my face. I placed a hand on the top of Q's head as I logged in. The camera I had would only show from my chest up, so if she behaved, we wouldn't have any issues.

I slipped my headphones on and waited for the stream to load. I wasn't going to stream any game play; she would be too distracting for that. Instead,

I would just do a little live catch-up with people and then call it a night. Quinlan had me eager to get this shit over with as quickly as possible so that I could go back to making her the center of my attention.

"Hey, guys," I said as people started flooding into the stream chat. That made Quinlan jump. She must have dozed off for a few minutes. I ran my fingers through her hair and saw her look up at me out of my peripherals. I ran my hand down her face, and she leaned into my palm, soaking up all the affection she could get. She acted starved for it, and I wondered when the last time was that anyone had treated her the way she deserved.

She shuffled around at my feet, getting more comfortable while I spoke to everyone that was joining. Once they realized I wasn't on to game, the requests started pouring in for all the freaky shit they wanted me to say. There were a few normal messages dotted in here and there, but most people were just sending me a shit ton of tokens to start putting my voice to good use.

"Oh, fuck," I groaned as I felt Quinlan's hands run over my thighs and across my crotch. It might have been dark in the room, but people watching would still be able to see if I looked down at her.

And I definitely couldn't say anything out loud to make her stop.

So her hands continued until I thought my dick was going to rip through my jeans it was so hard.

"Alright," I said with a shaky voice to the stream. Q's fingers popped open the button on my jeans and then slowly unzipped me. "How about we do something a little bit different this time." I was struggling to get full sentences out. She was going to have to slow down or this would be over far sooner than I wanted it to be.

"How about I talk us through an NSFW scenario instead of just spouting off random phrases that you guys throw my way, yeah?" I scanned the comments flooding in, and everyone seemed down. But that didn't really matter. Because the moment I felt her hand wrap around me, I was fucking gone.

I laid my head back and took a deep breath.

You can do this.

"You're under my desk while I'm streaming when you decide you want to give me some assistance. Your hands run up my thighs and across my crotch before freeing me and wrapping your soft hand around me."

I took a few deep breaths as she stroked me from base to tip. Her thumb ran along my slit, and I chanced a glance down only to see her lick the pad of her thumb where my precum had collected.

"Please?" she mouthed.

"Yes, baby," I murmured, turning my attention back to the stream. Or, at least, I tried. At that point, she had slipped her soft lips around me, and my mind could only focus on that.

"God, I love the way your mouth feels."

She had wrapped her mouth around me as far as she could go without gagging. No matter how badly I wanted to reach down and push her farther, I couldn't risk her making too much noise. I threaded my fingers through her hair and relished the feel of the silky strands.

I groaned as she sucked and licked me over and over.

"Do you like pleasing your master, baby girl? Do you like the feel of my hard cock slamming into the back of your throat while you gasp for air?" I asked as I pushed her just a bit farther down. I felt her throat constrict as she tried not to make any noise. "What a good little slut you are. Make me come, and I will reward you later."

Her sucking and stroking became more fevered.

"Fuck, you are a whore, aren't you? Only

whores are this good at cock sucking. The only thing you are good for, isn't it, pet?"

I felt my balls tighten and a familiar warmth begin to spread at the base of my spine and through my stomach. I gripped the front of her hair and pulled her off me before I could finish. I looked down at her as best I could. She held her mouth open, her chest panting, tongue still out, ready for me to let her finish me off. She couldn't even take her eyes off my dick.

What a fucking sight.

With my other hand, I gripped the base of my cock and smacked it against her tongue before letting go and watching her take me back in her mouth. I leaned my head back again, letting that warmth start to spread again.

"Keep doing that, baby. I'm going to finish in your mouth, and you are going to swallow every last drop. I want you to use that smart fucking mouth to milk me for all I'm worth."

I knew that what we were doing was so, so wrong. The people watching this stream didn't consent to this. They had no idea what they were actually watching. To them I was just acting out a scene. They had no clue that Q was beneath me, taking me in and out of her hot, wet mouth.

Fuck.

She was doing this thing with her tongue that was sending me over the fucking edge. My hips started to move in time with her mouth as she bobbed up and down, taking as much of me as she could. That fire was spreading through my entire body. My hands gripped on the sides of my chair so tightly I could feel them turning white.

"Jesus Christ, baby. Please," I found myself begging.

What the fuck.

I had never begged anyone for anything in my entire life. I didn't do the begging. They did. But with the way she was making me feel, and that tongue...my God.

"Please," I repeated, and I swear to God I could feel her smile against me.

Brat.

My balls tightened, my breathing hitched, and I groaned long and hard as my hips stuttered and pushed into her mouth, my hand keeping her head still and her mouth wrapped around me. I felt her swallow a few times, still sucking as my dick twitched in her mouth.

"Good girl," I said, a bit breathless. I didn't take a minute to look at any comments, any tokens I might have received, or to even say goodbye. They'd be fine. I had given them more than enough for tonight. I turned off the camera and the mic, signing off.

I pulled her up off the floor, lifting her onto my lap. She straddled me, and I groaned again as her slick heat pressed against me. I pulled off my mask, and before she could even register what I had done, I pulled her mouth to mine. She melted into me, and I let my hands slide down her body until they settled on her hips.

I could still taste myself on her, but I didn't care. It just made me want to swallow her whole. We were a clash of lips, teeth, and tongues. I sucked her tongue into my mouth and then let go to look at her face. Her lipstick was smeared, and her eyeliner was smudged. My dick twitched against her, wanting round two.

She took in my whole face and smiled, pushing my hoodie back off my head. I couldn't remember the last time I had let someone new look at me fully, knowing exactly who I was. But it was fucking freeing as hell, and I loved how she looked at me, drinking in every feature like she was committing it to memory. She kissed me softly.

"Hi, Jack."

"Come on, Curly Q," I laughed, landing a smack on her ass as I unclipped the leash from her collar and stood up, taking her with me. "Let's go for a swim."

She squealed as she wrapped her legs around my waist and her arms around my neck. I threw my mask down on the chair and carried her out back to my pool.

"You're stupidly rich, you know that?"

I snorted and opened the back door onto the patio. The sun was setting, and my outdoor lighting had turned on, making the backyard glow golden. I flipped a switch on the side of the house to turn the pool lights and waterfalls on.

"You can put me down. I can walk, and I know I'm not light."

"Shut the fuck up, you're beautiful," I said and gave her thick ass a squeeze. I meant it. I was attracted to every curve, every little roll, and every stretch mark she had on her body. Her tits were pressed up against my chest and with every step bounced against me. She was going to drive my dick insane.

She bit her lip in a smile and looked around.

"You cannot have made all this money just from gaming." She gave me a look, and I laughed.

Fair assumption, little one.

"Can you swim?"

"Of course I can swim," she said with her eyebrows scrunching together.

"Okay, good," I said and tossed her into the pool. I took my shirt off as she coughed and broke the surface.

"Jackass!" she yelled and pushed her hair out of her face. I smiled down at her and kicked off my jeans and boxers.

"Watch your mouth, pet."

"Get in here and make me."

I grinned down at her and watched her eyes roam over my body. My blood heated under her gaze, especially when she lingered just below my waist. She took her bottom lip between her teeth, and I jumped in next to her, making sure to make as big of a splash as possible.

"Asshole," she muttered as I came up beside her.

"You've got quite the mouth on you," I said, pulling her to me. I dipped my head back in the water to slick my hair out of my face. I kept it long, partially because it helped hide my face and partially because I liked it when girls had something to pull on.

Quinlan was staring at my mouth when I looked back at her.

"I like your lip piercing." Her arms wrapped around my shoulders, and I moved us over to the built-in bench so that I could sit her on top of me. I wasn't going to have sex with her yet, but I loved the sweet torture of her being pressed up against me.

"You used to have one," I said, rubbing my thumb across her lower lip where her scar was. Her lipstick was still smeared around her mouth like a bruise, and it only made her look more beautiful.

"I did. Not very professional though. I got rid of it a few years ago." Her fingers traced along the tattoos on my arm. "So," she said, leaning back to wet her hair as well. In the low light of the setting sun, it looked like liquid fire. Her breasts peeked out of the water, and it took all my willpower to not take them in my mouth. "What else do you do besides gaming to pay for all of this?" she asked, coming back up out of the water.

"Well, a few years ago, I came up with a very complicated and sought-after code and sold it to Microsoft. That's what paid for most of what you see. I also bought a string of clubs in LA and San Francisco with that money as an investment, and they are doing...very well." I could see her taking notes mentally as I spoke, still working even while she was playing. "I still stream and game because I enjoy it, not really because I have to anymore."

"And what would all of your adoring fans do without you?" She let out a little giggle, and I matched her smile. I let my hands fall from her hips to her thighs and gave them a squeeze.

"Adoring may be a strong word."

She shrugged. "So, the Joker, a faceless gamer and horny voice actor, is also Jack, a club owner and computer wiz."

I pulled her a bit closer, letting her heat settle against my length that was in a perpetual state of hardness with her around. She sighed, and I watched her skin glow rose gold in the setting sun.

"Basically," I said and then leaned forward and captured her mouth in mine. She ran her tongue across my lip ring. "What else do you want to know?" I asked, breaking from her lips only to grab them again. "You could ask me for anything right now and I think I'd give it to you."

She laughed into my mouth. "Okay," she said, breaking the kiss fully and pulling away so that I couldn't capture her again. She pushed off the seat and treaded out into the water. "What is something you want me to write about you?"

"What do you mean?" I asked as I watched her arms move through the illuminated water. The sun was setting quickly, almost completely below the horizon, which allowed her entire silhouette to be lit up underneath the warm water.

"If there was one thing you would want people to know about you, what would it be? Do you want me to paint you as this mysterious hard-ass?" She breathed a laugh. "Or do you want me to make you out to be the cinnamon roll that you are?"

"Cinnamon roll?"

"Yeah, you know. Squishy, sweet...tastes good..." She trailed off with a heated gaze.

"Squishy?" I asked with mock outrage as I advanced on her. She let out a loud laugh and tried to swim away, splashing water in my face to try and slow me down.

"Okay, okay!" she yelled as I caught up to her and pressed my fingers into her ribs, taking a correct guess that she would be ticklish. "Okay! Squishy was the wrong word!" I quit tickling her and pulled her back flush against my front. She took deep breaths, trying to calm down.

I pushed her hair off her shoulders and took her neck in my mouth, biting down hard enough to leave a bruise as my hand traveled lower and cupped her. She moaned, and I licked the bite.

"Is this what a squishy cinnamon roll would do?" She laid her head back on my shoulder, and a content smile spread across her lips. Even through the water, I could feel that she was wet for me. I let a finger push through her folds and softly circle her clit. Her entire body tensed as she took a deep breath.

"Okay, maybe I'll go with the mysterious hard-ass option," she said breathlessly. I smiled against her soft skin and kissed the mark I had left on her neck. My hand slipped free from between her thighs, and she groaned. "Definitely an ass though," she murmured.

"You were interviewing me," I said innocently. "I didn't want to be rude and distract you."

She turned around in my arms and looked up at

me. "Tell me about your parents. Where do you come from?"

I sighed and ran my hand through my hair. "My birth mom was never around. I never met her. She hung around for the first few months and then dipped. She was from Puerto Rico, and my dad always said he figured she went home to her family. She supposedly never wanted to be a mom. So I guess I'm just lucky I'm here." I shrugged when I saw Q's face drop.

"Jack," she murmured, her eyes sad. "I'm so sorry. I...I don't know what to say. That's awful."

"It's okay. Hard to miss someone you never knew. And my dad was more than enough of a parent."

"He's still around?"

"Definitely." My fingers traced little circles on every part of her skin. I couldn't get enough of it. It was going to be hard letting her walk out the door the next morning, knowing I wouldn't be able to taste her again. The deal was one night. One. But I wasn't sure now that it would be enough.

"So, where is he?" she asked, bringing me out of my thoughts.

"He's up in San Francisco now. He's some big-time lawyer up there."

"And he's supportive of you?" Her smile was warm, and I brought my thumb up to start wiping away the more stubborn lipstick that was still smeared.

"He is. He put himself through law school part-time once I was old enough to take care of myself after school. We struggled, but I never went without anything essential. And, like I said, once I was old enough, I got my own job and was able to get smart with money pretty quickly."

"I love that," she said, running her hands through my hair. "My parents are back in the Northeast, completely and totally not okay with the life I've chosen."

"Why's that?" I asked, frowning. "You seem to be doing okay."

"I'm doing more than okay, thank you. But I come from a very long line of very old money. And it was assumed and expected that I would follow in the footsteps of that money and become a doctor or a senator or something, I don't know," she finished, rolling her eyes. "But I love to write. I love meeting new people. And, as you can see," she said, gesturing to her tattoos. "I enjoy things senators and doctors aren't supposed to."

"Do you like other things senators and doctors

aren't supposed to, Quinlan?" Her eyebrows scrunched together in a silent question. "Like the things I was doing to you earlier? The things I was saying to you?" The sun was fully set, but I could still see the red creep across her cheeks. She looked away, but I grabbed her chin and pulled her attention back to me. I got within an inch of her lips, so close I could feel her breath across my own. "Did you like it, Quinlan?"

"Yes," she breathed.

With her confession that she liked everything I did to her, I carried her out of the pool, her luscious thighs wrapped tightly around me. Thank God I knew my way around my own place well enough that I could walk through it blind. Because she wasn't letting go of my mouth. And I didn't want her to.

I wrapped her hair around my fist and squeezed, trying to get as much of the excess water out of her hair as possible before going inside and taking her to my bedroom. I flicked one of the switches on the wall, and the room lit up a deep red. She broke the kiss and looked around and laughed.

"More LEDs? How cliché," she said a little breathlessly before crashing into my mouth again.

The head of my dick was barely touching her hot center, driving me fucking insane. I couldn't wait to sink into her and feel her clutch around me.

"Would you like your reward for being a good girl earlier?" I asked as I sat her down on my bed. She leaned back on her elbows and put one foot up on the bed, spreading her pussy open for me. I felt a growl roll through my chest. I was going to fucking devour her.

"Yes, please." That coy little smile was doing serious things to both my dick and my heart. If I didn't know any better, I was developing a little crush on the wild thing in front of me.

"Do you remember your safe words?"

"Yes."

"Good. Remember, you can use them at any time, and I will listen," I said, moving closer to her and taking her soft face in my hand.

"Give me your worst," she said with a fire in her eyes.

"Oh, babe," I said, stroking her still-wet hair off her face and shoulders. "This is your reward, not your punishment. This will be my best, not my worst." She tilted her head and smiled up at me before taking my lip into her mouth and teasing the ring there with her teeth.

"Give me your best, then, Joker." She gave me one last peck on the lips.

I walked around to the side of the bed and told her to scoot back and lie down. I took one wrist and cuffed her to the headboard. I had permanent ties attached to the top of my headboard and footboard, very well installed. Once she was in, there was no chance of her pulling free. As I walked around the bed, I tied both ankles so that she was spread wide open for me and then attached her other wrist to the headboard.

She tested the strength of the ties, tugging them a bit with her legs and arms, but she was barely able to move an inch. The cutest pathetic little noise came from her throat as she realized she was well and truly tied to the bed of someone she had only met a couple of hours ago.

Her chest began to rise and fall at a rapid rate.

"Hey, hey," I said in a low voice as I crawled up and over her body. She looked up at me with those big brown eyes, and my chest tightened. "I will take care of you. I will not harm you." I stroked her face. "Trust me. I'm going to make you see God, okay?" I asked, smiling down at her. Her breathing slowed, and she returned my smile.

"You can try," she countered.

"Oh, baby girl. I'm going to do far more than try." I reached out and took one of her nipples, rolling it between my finger and thumb before pinching it so hard she yelped and arched her back off the bed. I pulled on it until her heavy breast pulled up and away from her chest and then let it go and watched as her breast bounced back against her. Her hips moved and tried to get closer to me, wanting something to grind on. I was sure she was throbbing by now. I gave the other nipple the same attention and watched her writhe beneath me.

"I'll be right back, my little pet." I walked out of the room and back into my game room. Finding my headset where I left it on my desk, I picked it up and brought it back to the room with me. She raised her head as I walked back in, trying to see what I had left to get.

"Sensory deprivation can really heighten your orgasm because all of your focus is on sensation. I'm going to blindfold you and put these headphones on you. You won't be able to hear me or see me. You'll only be able to feel me. Okay, princess?"

Her eyes turned wary again, but I could see her pussy glistening in the red light from where I was. I knew she was so turned on she probably would've said yes to anything I suggested. She nodded.

I opened the drawer next to the bed and pulled out a blindfold. I was going to be back in that drawer in a moment to get a toy to play with as well, but she didn't need to know that. I slipped the blindfold over her eyes and then leaned over to kiss her cheek.

"Who does this pussy belong to?" I asked, cupping her drenched cunt and slipping two fingers in, hooking them to find that special little spot and pressing on it. She cried out and lifted her hips off the bed to meet the pressure I was giving her. "Whose fucking pussy is this?" I asked again, pulling my fingers out and pushing back in, hooking up for a second time.

"Yours!" she cried out, trying to grind her clit against the heel of my hand. "It's yours, please," she begged. "It's yours."

"Good girl, baby. Lie back and enjoy your reward." I slipped the headphones over her ears, effectively blocking out any noise.

I opened the drawer again, pulling out a wand and laying it at the bottom of the bed. I lay back over her, mindful to not let my cock graze any part of her. This wasn't for me. This was for her. She had been so trusting and so good for me.

She had made me beg for her mouth. Now I would make her beg for mine.

I kissed her, letting my tongue lazily meet hers before moving to her jaw and down her neck, kissing, nibbling, and licking. The faint taste of chlorine was on her skin, but the rest was all her. Her scent and taste was fucking intoxicating, and I couldn't stand to not touch her, taste her, or breathe her in.

She was addicting.

I made my way down her body and settled myself between her legs. I kissed my way up both of her thighs, stopping just before I made it to her bare sex. She smelled fucking incredible. I licked up both sides of her, smiling as she attempted to move closer to my mouth.

"Greedy," I murmured against her flesh even though she couldn't hear me.

Using my thumbs, I spread her open before me and then licked her from the bottom of her sweet little pussy all the way up to her clit before sucking it into my mouth. She gasped and pushed against my mouth. I hooked my arms under her legs and around her hips, pinning her to my face as I feasted on her like she was my last meal on earth.

"You taste so fucking sweet, baby," I said as I licked my lips, not wanting to miss a single drop of her. I sucked her clit back into my mouth, teasing it with my teeth and tongue. I set up a rhythm, working her up to her second orgasm of the evening. Her breaths were fast and short, and every little moan that escaped her lips was music to my ears. I ground my own hips into the mattress, trying to relieve some of my own need.

She groaned, took a deep breath, and then as I swirled my tongue in quick circles around her clit, she came apart. I dipped my tongue into her, lapping her up and losing my fucking mind over how tightly her orgasm was squeezing it.

Feeling her wrap around my cock was going to be the closest I had ever gotten to a spiritual experience.

As she came down, she was twitching, her chest heaving from trying to breathe. I gently flattened my tongue against her, making sure I didn't miss a drop but not overstimulating her...yet.

"Okay," she said between breaths. "I saw God. You were right. Holy shit." She was coming back down from her high, and I smiled. She thought we were done.

How cute.

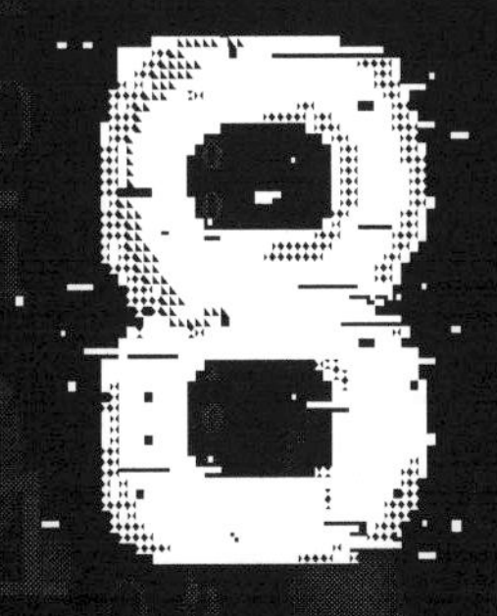

"Jack?" she asked, probably wondering why I hadn't taken the blindfold off yet. "Do not fuck with me," she warned in the cutest way ever. So threatening for someone so small. I smiled and clicked the wand on to the lowest setting before connecting it to her nipple.

She yelped, and her back arched off the bed. I watched her skin, still damp from the pool but also with sweat, pebble as her nipples stiffened even more. She was a whimpering, moaning mess, and it was so hot. Her squirming, quick breaths, and mewling noises were almost enough to make me finish without a single touch.

I moved the wand to her other nipple, and her hips bucked even harder, trying to find anything to grind on. I laughed and repositioned myself so that my knee was between her legs, just close enough that she could barely get her clit to make contact with my thigh. It would be just enough to be torture.

"Please, Jack," she moaned. God, I loved hearing my name on her lips. I never wanted it to stop. "If you want me to beg you for it, consider this begging!"

I smiled and placed my free hand between her thighs, inserting one and then two fingers. She was so wet that she was dripping onto the bed, and I was a little regretful that it was on the bed and not in my mouth.

I moved slowly in and out of her while I moved the wand down her stomach and around her hips. I settled it lightly on her clit, and she groaned deep in her throat.

"Did you just growl at me, princess?" I tsk'd and pressed the buttons a couple of times to turn it on high. I pushed it harder against her, and she really let out a scream then. I groaned, drinking in her sounds. I moved my fingers in and out at a steady, slow rhythm, hooking them inside her and massaging while I assaulted her clit with the vibrator.

I could hear how wet she was even over the sound of the wand and her moans. Her entire body was vibrating with pleasure, and I gazed down at her as her inner walls clenched around my fingers. She threw her head back into the mattress and screamed my name.

But I didn't slow down. I wanted to see her break. I wanted to see her body fall apart at my hands. I continued to press the vibrator to her swollen nub while fucking her with my fingers hard and fast.

"Jack, stop. Please. Please, oh my God, stop." She could barely breathe through the fire I knew was shooting through her body. She knew the safe word. And she wasn't saying it.

"Good girl, Quinlan," I said as I added another finger, filling her just a bit more. She cried out against the extra girth and bucked her hips, trying to get away from all the sensation. It was a lot when your body couldn't focus on anything else. When all your brain had to listen to was touch, it tended to get a little overpowering. "Yes, baby girl. Come again for me. Come on, baby."

"Jack!" she screamed as she came again, squirting and clenching around me so tightly I couldn't do anything but ride it out with her. I turned off the wand, not wanting it to become too painful, and slowly pulled my fingers from her now very tired cunt. My ego fucking soared at the sight of her soaking my bed.

I did that.

"Told you you'd see God," I said out loud to myself.

I leaned over her red and swollen pussy, and she jumped when she felt my cool breath on her sex. I pressed the flat of my tongue across her engorged clit and then sucked it gently into my mouth.

I lazily licked inside her, down to her ass, and nibbled on her outer lips. I sucked her into my mouth one more time, causing her to nearly jump out of her skin before positioning myself over her.

My dick was dripping, and I was so hot and ready for her, but it wasn't my turn yet. She needed a break. She needed food and a drink. She needed care. And I wasn't going to be selfish and use her past the point of pleasure.

I let my body rest on hers and slipped the headset off slowly, letting her get accustomed to having her hearing back. I nuzzled my face into her neck and nipped at her ear.

"Hi, baby girl," I whispered. She breathed in and turned her face toward me. I gave her a small kiss before gently tugging the blindfold off her eyes. She blinked a few times and then met my gaze.

"Hi," she said, smiling over at me. I reached up above us and released her arms. Doing the same with her ankles, I started to remove the sheets from the bottom of the bed.

"Roll over for a sec," I said once I got all the corners up. She rolled over onto the soft mattress protector, and I pulled the sheets completely off. She rolled back onto the bed.

"I'm sorry."

"For what?" I asked as I threw the blankets on the floor—I would deal with those later—and pulled a fresh blanket out from a drawer.

"The mess I made on your sheets. That's embarrassing," she groaned and rolled over onto her stomach to hide her face.

"There's nothing to be sorry for or embarrassed about," I said, crouching down at the side of the bed to look at her. "I should be thanking you for the compliment. There's nothing hotter than knowing I made you so satisfied you left a puddle on my sheets." She groaned again, turning bright red, and closed her eyes. "Hey," I said, tapping her cheek. "I'm serious. I've never been his hard in my entire fucking life, Quinlan."

She opened her eyes and rolled them before moving to sit up.

"Nope," I said, stopping her. "Stay here a second. I'm going to go get something to clean you up, and then you get whatever you want to eat."

I laid the blanket on the side of the bed and made my way to my master suite to wet a washcloth with warm water. I needed to clean her up and cover her fucking body with that blanket so I could get rid of my raging hard-on. I slipped on some sweats and tucked myself into the waistband until it decided to calm down.

Walking back over to the bed, I spread her legs and wiped her clean before throwing the cloth onto the pile of dirty sheets.

"Thank you," she said sleepily as I covered her with the blanket.

"What are you hungry for? I don't really have any food in the house, but I will order you whatever you want. We're going to need some calories to make it through the rest of the night." She gave me a look, and I shrugged. "What? If you think I'm not keeping you here until the sun comes up, you've lost your mind. Now, what do you want?"

"Pizza," she laughed. "Just pepperoni, please."

I went off in search of wherever I had left my

phone and let her rest. When I finally found it, I ignored all of the notifications and ordered the pizza. When I was done, I took a few minutes to read through everything I had missed. There were a few emails from the managers of my nightclubs just checking in or sending reports.

I checked in on all of my social media outlets. A lot of people were asking for a repeat performance of tonight. I laughed to myself. *Same*, I thought. A few texts from my friends reminding me of our plans to meet at one of my clubs downtown. I had been too swept up in Quinlan to remember those plans.

I was about to shoot off an excuse to them about why I couldn't make it when I had an idea. We weren't supposed to meet for another couple of hours. And taking her out for a few hours could be fun. Thoughts of her in a tight-as-sin outfit, on my arm, flaunting her in front of everyone...fuck, my boner was never going to go down.

I made my way back into my bedroom to find her fast asleep. I crawled under the blanket behind her and pulled her into my body. She rolled over and rested her head on my arm and threw one of her legs over my hips. She could barely open her eyes.

"Pizza?"

"On its way. Sleep. I'll wake you up when it's here, don't worry," I answered.

"You want to know something?" she asked, burying her face into my chest. "You're going to think I'm lying to make you feel like some sort of god or something," she laughed. "But I swear I'm not. A guy has never been able to make me finish."

"I...what?" I asked, shocked.

"Yeah," she yawned. "I just always faked it to get them to stop trying. And here you are, giving me three out-of-body experiences in the span of a few hours." I breathed her in, trying to find the right words to say. But I didn't have to. She had fallen back asleep.

No one had ever in her entire life made her finish. What kind of fuckwads were out there? I would never understand men and their inability to care about anything other than getting their dicks wet and then leaving. Not bothering to check on their partner and see if they had enjoyed it as well.

Shit, I could understand finishing first. It happened to the best of us. But you still made sure she got hers before fucking off home.

I sighed.

"Give me strength," I said quietly to myself as I rubbed my eyes. I pulled my phone out of my pocket and set an alarm for thirty minutes to make sure I would be awake when the pizza arrived. I shoved the phone under my pillow and closed my eyes, falling asleep to the comforting sound of Q's quiet breaths.

"I want you to come out with me tonight," I said as she finished her pizza. I was sitting behind her on the couch, rubbing her back, when I decided that little fantasy of mine with her dressed up on my arm was actually going to happen.

"Where?" she asked, turning around and looking a little surprised.

"My club downtown."

She looked herself up and down. "You want me to go to a nightclub, looking like this?"

I smiled and peeled myself away from her. "No, obviously not." I had already thought about this. "I'll run you by your place, let you get ready, and then we'll go. I had plans to meet some of my friends for a bit tonight but got too wrapped up in you and forgot. But I kind of like the idea of taking you out and getting a chance to see you all dolled up and on my arm."

"Okay," she laughed. "Whatever. I live over in Brookdale. Is that okay?"

"Yep!" I said and stood up off the couch. "I'm going to go take a quick shower so that I don't smell like chlorine, and then we will head over to yours, yeah?"

"Okay." She smiled a bit wider. Maybe she liked the idea of being on my arm, too.

Forty-five minutes later, I pulled into the parking garage of her apartment complex and followed her up to her twelfth-floor apartment. It was bigger than what I had expected for a writer, but I guess she hadn't been lying when she said she was doing perfectly fine on her own.

"Remote is on the stand next to the couch. Make yourself comfortable. I'll try to be quick."

I looked around at her open apartment. She had plants everywhere. Some were hanging from the ceiling, some were sitting on little stands, and others just spaced out on the floor. Her home had so much personality it made mine seem stark and cold. She had an emerald velvet couch and a multicolored rug that almost took up the entirety of her living room floor.

When I heard the shower turn on, I ventured into her room and saw more of the same rich fabrics and fucking plants everywhere. Was I fucking some kind of garden fairy? A green witch?

Jesus Christ.

I opened her closet and sifted through all of her clothing until I found the section that seemed to hold all of her dresses. There was one that immediately caught my eye. It was the softest satin and a deep forest green that would look amazing with her hair. I pulled it out and laid it on her bed and then went on the hunt for shoes.

At the back of her closet on the floor were black strappy ones that I knew were going to do wonders for her ass. Looking at her other shoes, I guessed she wasn't a huge fan of heels. Oh, well. I was more than willing to carry her anywhere we went.

She walked out of the bathroom in a cloud of steam, her skin still flushed from the shower. I spotted the bite mark on her neck that was starting to bruise and smiled. If that didn't scream she was mine, I didn't know what would. I had let her take the collar off before leaving the house, even though I would've liked to see everyone's reactions to that.

Mine, I thought again as she dropped the towel and sauntered toward me. Her hair was wet and wavy, falling across her shoulders and dripping water down the valley between her breasts. I hadn't been that possessive of another person in a long time, and it started a little thread of anxiety in my chest. I wasn't the easiest person to deal with when I started down that road.

My dick stirred yet again.

"Please put these fucking clothes on before I throw you against the wall and fuck you until you scream and wake up your neighbors."

She grinned and looked down at the bed next to us. "You picked out my outfit?" she asked.

"Yes. I want to see you in green."

"Green it is, then. But you may have to carry me by the end of the night. I've never been great in heels. I'm clumsy at the best of times." She walked over to her dresser and started sifting through bras and underwear.

"You may wear a bra. You may not wear underwear." She looked at me over her shoulder, and I took a moment to admire her pert ass. "I want access to you at all times." She rolled her eyes but only pulled out a bra. Grabbing the dress off the bed, she turned and walked back into the bathroom.

"I'll be fast," she said and closed the door. I was probably going to look underdressed next to her, but I had never really cared about that. Even though I was the owner of the club, I was known to show up in my signature black boots, black jeans, and black T-shirt.

After some time had passed, the door creaked open, and I sat up and drank her in. She had made her hair pin straight, and against the dark green of the dress, it almost looked purple. Her makeup was done dark and heavy, and I loved it. Against her pale skin, it made her look luminous.

And that dress.

That fucking dress.

All of her tattoos were out on display, and the way it hugged her hips had me reeling. It stopped at her midthigh, but the slit went almost up to her hip. That was going to make it very easy for me to slide my hand in there at any given moment.

"Like it?" she asked, seeming a bit shy.

"That's an understatement. You're going to be the hottest person in this club tonight," I said as I picked up her shoes and then knelt in front of her. She held on to the dresser next to her, and I lifted one of her feet and slid it into her shoe. I clasped the buckle and kissed her thigh before moving to the other and doing the same thing.

When I looked up at her, she had her eyes closed. I kissed her leg a bit higher up and watched her chest rise and fall a bit quicker. I ran my nose up across her soft skin that the slit in her dress was showing off. Her hand came to rest in my hair.

"Don't start something you can't finish," she said as her grip on my hair turned rough. The quick burst of pain made my stomach tighten in the best way. She looked down at me.

"Do you like seeing me on my knees for you, pet? Did you like it when my cock was in your mouth and I was begging you for it? Do you like that you can make me weak?"

She pulled my head back, and I smiled. I had never let anyone dominate me in any way, shape, or form. Not even in the small way Quinlan was doing in that moment.

But as she gazed down at me with that all-too-familiar spark in her eyes, I thought maybe I would be willing to see what it was like to be on the receiving end of that fire. I growled deep in my chest and ran my hands up the backs of her legs until I found her ass. Cupping it, I squeezed until she flinched.

I stood and kissed her on her neck.

"It's going to be a miracle if I survive this night," she said under her breath as we made our way out of her apartment.

"By the way," I started, holding the door open for her. "What's with all the plants? How do you keep them alive? Are you a witch? A little garden fairy?"

She threw her head back in a laugh. I really, really liked making her laugh.

"I just like taking care of things," she said after she stopped laughing. "Trust me, I killed plenty before I got the hang of it."

She clung to my arm to keep herself upright as we made our way back downstairs and to the car. She even had to lean into me slightly to make sure she wasn't rolling any ankles. I offered to just pick her up and carry her down, but she pushed me away and told me to save it for later on.

On our way, I texted to my friend Wes as I closed the passenger-side door.

Wes: Our? Who are you bringing?

You have other friends? Is this a girl?!

Behave.

I smiled at her as I started the car.

"Ready?"

"As I'll ever be." I shifted and pulled out of the garage, hoping this last-minute decision wasn't a mistake.

10

I left my car with the valet and escorted her inside and upstairs to the VIP area, where all my friends were already seated. Taking her to her apartment and letting her get ready made us a little late. Probably didn't help that I had pulled over to finger fuck her to climax on the way. I couldn't help myself. That dress was the sweetest kind of torture.

"So do any of these people know about your little alter ego?" she asked as we made our way up the stairs.

"They do. They've been my friends since before I started it up."

"There you are!" Wes shouted as he ran up and pulled me into a hug. "She's hot, bro," he said into my ear before literally pushing me out of the way to look down at Quinlan.

"Hi," she said, smiling up at him. "I'm Quin."

"Quin!" he said as he stooped down and picked her up in his arms. I rolled my eyes and watched them, trying to not let it get to me that his hands were on her. He was my best friend, after all. And it's not like she was actually mine. It shouldn't bother me.

She squealed and threw her head back in laughter after she got over the initial shock of being picked up by a bear. Wes didn't seem to ever remember how big he actually was. He was a few inches taller than my six feet, and he was built like a damn bodybuilder. Wes was a bounty hunter. And he was damn good at it. He was someone you wanted on your side in a fight.

"My name is Wes. It's so good to meet you! Welcome to the group!" He squeezed her one more time before gently setting her back down on her feet.

"Nice to meet you, too, Wes," she said, trying to make sure her dress hadn't ridden up. She slinked her arm through mine and leaned into me. I let loose a breath I hadn't quite realized I was holding during that entire exchange.

"Come on, come on," he said, motioning us to follow him over to the rest of the group. "These guys won't bite, even though they may look like they do." He looked up at me, and I raised an eyebrow. "Okay, maybe we do bite. But not people we like." He paused and his eyes moved down to her with a wicked grin. "Unless you ask for it." He winked at her.

"She won't," I answered for her.

He looked back up at me and smiled knowingly. *Bastard.* I should've known he was doing that to get a reaction. He was testing the waters to see if I would be territorial. I felt Quinlan gaze up at me, but I stared straight ahead, smiling at my group of friends as we approached the table.

"Guys," Wes addressed the table before I could. "This is Quin, and we are going to be on our best behavior around her, or Jack here might kick all of our asses."

I rolled my eyes and pulled out a chair for her to sit in. I sat next to her and started introductions.

"Wes you met," I said loud enough over the music for everyone to hear. "He's a bounty hunter. And Greg," I said, pointing to the blond who didn't have an inch of skin not covered in tattoos, "he's a software developer and a hothead. He's normally the one to get us all in trouble." He rolled his eyes at me but smiled at Quinlan.

"Nice to meet you, Quin," he said.

"This little fucker is Owen. He's a trust fund baby."

"I am not a trust fund baby!" he countered. "My parents just happen to be very rich," he said, winking at Quinlan. "And they gave me businesses to run." When he said "businesses," he did air quotes.

"They're restaurants," I said to her. "Don't let him convince you he's some big-time drug lord or something. He runs a string of Asian restaurants." He scoffed. "We are kind of convinced at this point, though, that he's part of a mafia family," I murmured into her ear when Owen looked away. "He's never confirmed nor denied that one." She grinned.

"And this is Hudson," I said, nodding to my last friend sitting to my right. "But everyone calls him Pyro. He has a not-so-little obsession with fire."

"Nice to meet you, Quin," he said, extending his arm and shaking her hand. She glanced down, but to her credit, her eyes didn't linger on the multiple burn scars covering his hands.

"He's the little brother of the group and acts like

it, too. He's a drummer in a band and does absolutely nothing else."

"What do you do, Quin?" Greg asked from across the table.

"I'm a writer," she called out. "I work for The Lead, an online gaming magazine. I've also started writing some stories on the side. I'd like to become an author one day." I looked down at her and smiled, putting my arm on the back of her chair. The waiter came up behind us.

"What do you want?" I asked her. "What do you like?"

She looked me up and down with a coy little smile. "Anything sweet."

"Yeah, I bet you do," Owen said. I kicked him under the table as Quinlan laughed, and he spit out his drink, giving me a glare.

"Behave," I said, pointing in his direction.

I ordered for us both and leaned back in my chair, switching my attention from people watching to watching Quinlan. She laughed and chatted with my friends like she had known them for years.

After a few drinks, my arm had fallen from the back of her chair to her shoulders. We had started the night with our chairs a bit apart from each other, but when I looked down, they were pressed flush. I couldn't remember doing that, but it didn't surprise me. Ever since she had walked into my life, I had felt the need to be as near her as possible. She looked over at me and caught me staring.

Her hand found my thigh, and I blinked, trying to turn my attention back to the group and whatever the hell they had been talking about since I had zoned out. Thank God Quinlan seemed to be holding her own with them because I was no help.

"Yeah," she was saying, nodding her head at Hudson. "I didn't really like it. Well, okay, wait. I liked it, but I didn't like the lessons."

"No one likes the lessons," he said. "I learned how to play on my own. Taking lessons takes all the fun out of it. Makes it feel more like an obligation and less like something you enjoy."

"You play drums?" I asked her, a bit shocked.

"Ah, welcome back to the conversation," Owen said while Quinlan laughed.

"No, I took piano lessons as a kid." She turned her gorgeous eyes on me, and she looked so fucking happy I wanted to grab her face and kiss the life out of her.

"Not to break up the lovefest going on over there," Owen said, sitting his drink down on the table. "But I think it's time to let Quin have some fun. Let's go dance."

"Yes!" Wes shouted and stood up with Owen and Hudson. Greg stayed firmly in his seat. The last thing he would be caught doing is dancing. *Grumpy bastard.* Not that I could say much. It wasn't my favorite thing either, but to see Quinlan's body moving to the music, pushing up against me?

Fuck.

"Sir?" I looked up and saw Anders hovering behind me. He was an older guy, late thirties, and smart as hell with numbers. He came highly recommended by Owen's family, so I had scooped him up as soon as possible when I bought up the clubs. This one was his home base, but he was always traveling around to all of them, checking in, and keeping shit straight.

"Anders, please," I said, rubbing my eyes. "I've asked so many times. Please don't call me sir. My name is Jack."

"Um, Jack," he started over. "Derek told me you were here. We've got some issues related to the business and thought that maybe you would want to go ahead and look everything over while you were here instead of having to come all the way back down here tomorrow?"

I looked down at Q and then over at Wes. He nodded.

"Go take care of shit, I've got her."

"Because she wouldn't be safe with me?" Owen asked.

"No one is safe with you," Hudson answered. "Who knows what kind of shady shit you're into."

"As if you're one to talk, Pyro," Wes chimed in. "You fuck anything that moves."

Quinlan laughed and watched their banter back and forth. Hudson looked down at her and pulled a toothpick out of his back pocket and stuck it in his mouth. It was a nervous habit he'd had for as long I knew him. He was always chewing on the damn things.

"Don't believe him, darlin'. I'll be on my best behavior, I promise," he said.

She swayed a step as we stood, and I looked down at the table. She'd had quite a few drinks, and as small as she was, I wasn't surprised she was already feeling the effects.

"You okay?" I asked. "It won't take long at all, and they'll take care of you. They may look and act like a band of misfits, but they know I will kill them if they don't."

"Quite literally," Greg said before looking over at me. "I'll keep an eye from up here."

"I'm fine." She gave me a playful little shove. "I'll be in a big badass man sandwich. What can go wrong?"

A lot, I thought to myself. We seemed to attract trouble everywhere we went. Ever since we all found each other, we were known as the guys to steer clear of. Not sure if it was Greg's hot temper, Owen's assumed mafia background, Wes's bounty hunting, Hudson's obsession with fire, or my possessiveness, but we were always having to bail each other out.

"Fine," I said, relenting and giving her a quick kiss on the top of her head. I looked at each of my friends. "Come get me if anything happens."

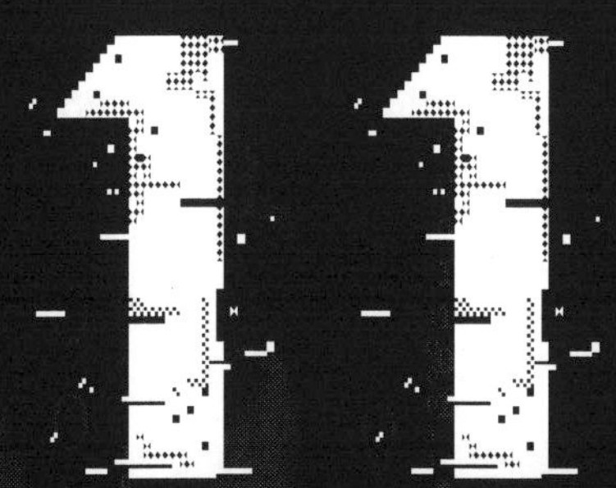

11

WES

"Does a lot of bad stuff tend to happen at this club or just around you guys?" she asked me as we made our way down to the dance floor.

"Honestly?" I laughed. "Us."

"Good to know," she said, laughing as well.

The truth was, trouble did tend to find us even when we weren't looking for it. And yes, sometimes we did go looking for it. I looked down at her out of the corner of my eye as she gripped my arm in one hand and Owen's in the other. Hudson was following close behind, looking around the dance floor and twisting that stupid toothpick around.

She was gorgeous. No wonder Jack had decided to keep her close. We all knew what Jack was into, and it surprised me to look down at this little slip of a thing and imagine her being down with all that shit.

Don't get me wrong, we all had our vices. Pyro had his fire and his women. Owen had whatever the fuck he got up to with his family when we weren't around. Greg had a serious thing for knives. I pitied the woman that caught his attention and kept it one day.

And me? I had my fighting. I couldn't go more than a few days without beating the absolute shit out of someone. Whether it was legal or illegal, I was always in the ring trying to get my kicks. Speaking of, it had been far too long since I had hit something.

"Greg is watching," Owen said down to her, bringing me out of my thoughts. "Don't let anyone but us touch you, or he's going to report that back to Jack, and Jack will not be happy."

I saw her eyebrows scrunch together in a silent question.

Oh, I thought. *She has no idea what she has gotten herself into.*

"Look," I said to her, stopping all of us at the

bottom of the stairs. "Jack may seem like a sweet guy, and he is, don't get me wrong. But once he sees something he likes, he's like mama bear with her cubs."

Pyro laughed at that. "It's true," he said. "Horrible analogy, but yeah. He can be extremely possessive."

"He's only known me for a total of like five hours. And we aren't together," she protested. "It's just a one-night type of thing. We're just hanging out."

"Yeah," Owen said. "Keep telling yourself that. But we all saw how he was looking at you at the table. And you were looking at him like a kid in a candy shop."

"Either way," I said, butting in before they talked themselves into a hole and he spooked her. "You're his for the night, at least. And he isn't going to like someone else touching what's his. So just stay between all of us okay?"

"Uh, okay," she said, her cheeks turning red under all the attention. "Are you guys going to dance with me though? It's going to be a bit awkward if you all just stand in a circle around me while I dance by myself."

"Wes and Pyro will dance with you. Greg has

eyes from upstairs; I'm going to be the eyes downstairs," Owen answered.

She rolled her eyes and smiled. "Fine, whatever. Enough chitchat. Let's go. You guys can be like my own little harem tonight."

We all barked out a laugh, and I threw my arm around her shoulders. "Yes, ma'am. Lead the way."

Owen went off to stand next to the bar with a clear sight straight to where we were in the middle of the dance floor. Pyro and I danced with her, taking turns spinning her, holding her up so that she didn't break an ankle, and letting her somewhat innocently grind up against us.

Her face was lit up constantly with the biggest smile I had ever seen. It made her eyes sparkle, and it was infectious to be around. Even Owen was smiling at her from the sidelines. I would never tread on one of my friends' toes, but I was jealous as fuck that this creature had made her way to him instead of me.

When it was my turn to take her and let her lean on me while she danced, another girl with white-blonde hair sidled up next to Pyro and stole his attention. He looked over at me, and I nodded. Everything seemed fine. The club was relatively chill for once. I didn't even see anyone coming near us that could've given us a fair fight.

But then next thing I knew, Quin had been knocked free of my arms and she was on the floor, her dress up around her naked hips as she quickly tried to pull it down before anyone saw anything. She was pretty quick about it, but anyone paying attention had just received an eyeful.

Shit.

I whipped my head around to find the culprit while Pyro literally pushed the pretty girl off him and dropped to the floor to help Quin stand back up. My eyes landed on a Chad that was staring down at her bare legs and laughing.

"Oh, you fucked with the wrong woman," I yelled over the music. His eyes swiveled up to me, and he snorted. That was not a reaction I was used to getting from men. Normally, they took one look at me and backed down. I was a pretty big guy and had a way of making myself seem larger when I needed to.

"Come on, bro," he said, taking another swig from his cheap-ass beer. "She's just some slut that didn't even bother to wear panties. Asking for it, if you ask me."

"Wrong answer," Owen said, suddenly beside me.

"Get her out of here," I said to Pyro. He picked her up, careful not to expose her to anyone else around us, and carried her off. I saw her mouth moving, but the music swallowed up her protests. My entire body thrummed with adrenaline.

"This really isn't your night, pal," I said when he realized both Owen and I were not on his side of things. He looked around frantically, probably trying to see if his friends were going to come to his rescue. It didn't matter if they did. Greg would have already seen and let Jack know there was an issue. He'd be out soon with Anders to shut it down.

"Come on, man," he stuttered. "I was just messing around."

He started to back up, but Owen reached out and grabbed him by the collar to keep him within our grasp. A few men who I assumed were his friends came over, asking what was going on.

I smiled.

Finally, I thought.

I took a deep breath and swung, my fist connecting with the guy's jaw and sending him flying out of Owen's grip. He was out cold on the ground when I looked around to his friends.

"Boss man is going to be out soon to ruin our fun, lads. So better make this fast. Who's next?"

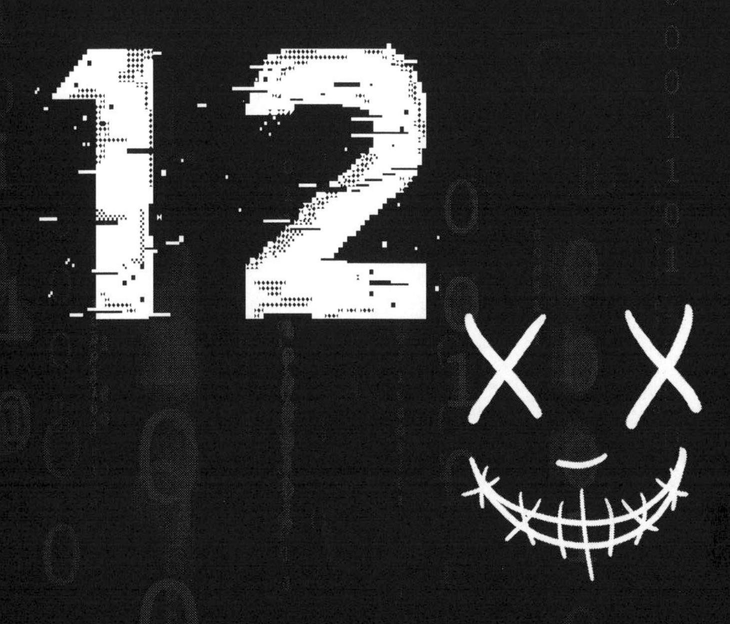

12

JACK

It was a fucking flurry of fists on the dance floor. People were scattering, trying to get out of the way unscathed. Greg had come to get me as soon as he saw Q fall to the floor. I looked around, trying to find where she had gone. Owen and Wes were in the middle of everything, and Greg was running down the stairs to join in.

I really should have known better than to think we could have one fucking night without someone kicking off. I wouldn't have been complaining on a normal night. But this wasn't a side I had wanted her to see of me yet.

I didn't see Hudson anywhere and hoped Wes

had been in his right mind enough to get Hudson to take her away somewhere and make sure she wasn't hurt from the fall. Guilt pulled at my chest for making her wear those heels even after she had told me she would struggle in them.

Selfish.

"Shut. It. Down," I told Anders, who had followed us out and still stood next to me on the balcony. "We don't need any more bad fucking press." He nodded and walked off while I went down to find the one that had pushed her.

I didn't give a fuck about anyone else in the fray. I wanted that one guy. The one who had touched her. The one that had had his hands on her. The one that probably saw her bare cunt on display.

He touched what was mine.

"Who was it?" I yelled over the noise of the music and the sounds of fists on flesh. The strobe lights were distorting everything around me, making it hard to focus on more than one person at a time.

"On the floor! Blond!" Wes shouted back, smiling as he spat blood out onto the floor. I rolled my eyes. Someone was going to have to clean all of this up, and it wasn't making it easier on them. I turned my attention from him to pushing people out of my way until I saw the culprit of this entire thing lying on the floor, just waking up as someone tripped over him. He tried to sit up.

I placed my boot on his shoulder and shoved. He fell back to the floor and looked up at me. The look on his face told me he was two seconds away from shitting himself.

"You touched my girl?" I asked, staring down at him. He swallowed and looked around for help. "Did you look at her bare pussy when she fell?" He shook his head back and forth. I cracked my neck to the side and crouched down to his level.

"I didn't, man, I swear!"

I smiled and twisted the rings on my fingers before looking back up at him. "I think you're lying," I said calmly. "I don't like liars, Chad." I didn't know if that was his name, but I didn't give a fuck. Mr. Frat Boy didn't flow off the tongue as nicely. "Didn't your mother ever teach you that the punishment is always worse when you lie?"

"Okay, okay, man. Yes, I looked at her when she fell."

"She's beautiful, isn't she?" I asked with an unkind smile on my face. He nodded and started to try and crawl back away from me. "She isn't yours to look at though, Chad. She's mine. And you need to learn to respect others' property." I stood just as he managed to turn and start to stand up again.

I swung out and kicked him in the ribs. He fell over on his back, gripping his side where I knew I had just cracked at least one of his ribs. The music stopped, and all the lights went out. Anders was finally shutting everything down. I felt people start scattering under the cover of darkness. I took the opportunity to straddle him on the floor and land a punch across the side of his face, my rings cutting slits into his skin.

"Everyone out! Now!" Anders said over the PA system before the lights came on, flooding the entire club with fluorescent lights. The floor was quickly emptying, and I took a second to dig through his pockets and find his wallet. Pulling out his ID, I snapped a picture of it with my phone.

"Wow," I said, sliding it back into his pocket. "Your name actually is Chad." He looked up at me through his eye that was already starting to swell shut. "Well, surprise, bro. I'm the owner of this club, and you've been officially banned."

I climbed off him and nudged him with my boot. He got the message and scurried up onto his feet and made his way out of the club, clutching his side.

"Send us the hospital bill. It's on us if you keep your mouth shut and your hands off women!" I shouted after him.

Wes groaned to my left, and I looked over at him. His knuckles were bloody, he had a wide smile on his face, and his chest was heaving. I rolled my eyes. He loved a good fight, and by the looks of the assholes that were crawling out of here, it had been a while since he had had one.

"You should've beat him into silence," he said.

"He has to protect his precious gamer hands," Owen laughed, kicking a guy toward the door, literally.

"This is not what I meant when I said look after her," I said, groaning into my hands.

"I saw him walking towards you guys from the balcony. He had his sights on her. He knew what he was doing," Greg said, wiping his bloody nose on his sleeve.

"Who has her?" I asked them all.

"Pyro carried her off the floor before it got out of control. I'm guessing he took her to one of the offices in the back where he could lock the door," Wes answered.

"Will you guys please help Anders get shit under control and get the cleanup process started?"

"I'll make some calls to make sure this doesn't get out," Owen said, walking back up to the balcony, taking the steps two at a time. I assumed by "making calls," he meant to his family. I had never asked questions, but when it came to that kind of shit with my clubs, he was always able to keep things under wraps. Because yes, shit like this did seem to happen far too often when we all got together.

"We'll go help Anders," Wes said.

"Go make sure she's okay," Greg said before I started stalking off to the back where all of the private offices were.

"Pyro?" I shouted down the hallway. My office door at the far end of the hallway creaked open.

"In here, bud," he called back and stepped out, shutting the door behind him. "She's fine," he said as I walked down toward him, probably with a look that could kill plastered across my face. He laughed a bit as I got closer. "Bro, don't go in there looking like that, or you're going to scare the shit out of her. She's fine. Her ankle is just a bit twisted, is all. And she's a little embarrassed."

I took a deep breath. I needed to get my shit together. I was coming apart at the seams over a girl I had just met. This wasn't normal. Normal people didn't get obsessed like this. She probably was scared shitless in there. I highly doubted anyone had ever reacted like that to her just falling down on a dance floor.

If no one had ever even taken the time to make her finish, I doubted anyone had ever cared enough to stick up for her.

I half groaned, half growled as I stood outside the door with Hudson. I looked at him while I paced back and forth, trying to kick the adrenaline out of my system.

"You've known her for all of, what? Five hours?" I threw him a look that told him to shut up. I knew where he was going, and I didn't feel like going down that road. "Only one night, she told us."

"It's only one night," I agreed.

"Mmm." He nodded. "So one of your little games you play? You haven't had one of those in a while. But she seems different. You've never brought anyone else out. Especially not a girl that's supposed to just be hanging around for a night. Shouldn't you have just kept her home and fulfilled all of your freaky kinks?"

"Pyro," I said with an edge of warning to my voice.

"Just saying, man. Maybe it's time to stop

fucking around and try the whole dating thing for once."

"That takes a lot of trust," I admitted.

"I realize that for you there's a lot more riding on it because of your privacy needs, but you can't just hide away your entire life because you like talking dirty online and playing games behind a mask." I grunted. "Maybe you've met your match."

"I've not even known her a day," I countered.

"Sometimes you don't have to."

"For someone who flits from one girl to another as often as you change underwear, you're kind of a romantic."

He laughed and patted me on the shoulder.

"I don't wear underwear," he said into my ear. I groaned and pushed him away as he cackled.

"Go help the others. I'm taking her home."

"Yeah, you are!" he yelled back, wagging his eyebrows, and jogged down the hall.

When I walked into my office she was lying on the couch, her foot propped up on a pillow and one of my hoodies I had left here laid over her lap. She looked up at me when I walked in and eyed me nervously.

"Are you okay, princess?" I asked, squatting down next to the couch. She nodded and looked down at my hands that were clasped in front of me. Grabbing them, she pulled me toward her until I sat next to her on the couch, her fingers running over the blood on my own.

"Do you guys always beat the shit out of people, or was that just for my benefit?" she asked with a smile.

"We can be a bit hotheaded." She laughed and

laid her arm across my waist. "Are you ready to leave?"

"Or," she said, sitting up and moving carefully to straddle me, "we could finish what you've been starting all night." I pushed my hands through her hair and out of her face. Her lips came down on mine. Her tongue ran across my lip ring, and she moaned as she moved her hips against mine.

"Look what you've done to me," she said, grabbing my hand and pushing it under her dress and onto her sex. I kept my eyes on her as we continued to kiss in between her words. The desperation in her voice was about to send me over the fucking edge.

"Did you make him bleed?" she asked as she pressed one of my fingers and one of her own inside her. Together we moved slowly between her folds, soaking both of our hands.

Fuck, this is hot.

"Yes," I groaned into her mouth, "Yes, I made him bleed for you, baby." I could have sworn she got even wetter at that admission than she had been already.

Where the fuck had this girl come from? She was a writer, dressed up in blazers and soft makeup during the day, and then this dark, wild creature at night, baring that side of her only to me.

"I want you inside of me," she said, still riding both of our hands like her damn life depended on it. "I want to see if you can make me come around your cock the way you can with your fingers." She pushed us farther into her for emphasis. "And your mouth," she said, biting down hard on my lower lip.

Her hand left mine and popped open my jeans, pulling down the zipper and reaching down to release me from my boxers. Her soft hand gripped my shaft, and I pulled my finger free of her wet heat and brought it to my mouth, sucking it clean while she watched me. Her eyes were black and hooded with lust while she stroked me gently, too fucking gently, from base to tip and back again.

She was teasing me, letting the tip of my dick roll against her clit while just barely touching me. Both of my hands came up around her throat, and she smiled as she struggled to take in air.

"Put me inside of you, princess," I demanded. "Ride my cock like the good little girl you are. And when I finally let you come, I want you to scream my name so loudly everyone in this fucking club hears you. Do you understand me?"

As an answer, she lined my head up with her

cunt and dropped down with such force I thought I was going to be a one-pump wonder.

"Jesus fucking Christ!" I growled, my hands dropping to her hips and holding her still. I leaned my forehead against hers and closed my eyes. "You feel so fucking good, baby. You're so tight."

And she was. Fuck me, she was so tight. She fit around me like a god had molded her just for me, and even though I held her hips still, her inner walls squeezed me. When I opened my eyes, she was smiling. She knew exactly what the fuck she was doing.

"I'm so full," she said in a pitiful little voice that had my dick twitching inside of her. I wrapped my arms around her and slowly started grinding her hips back and forth, letting her clit take all the friction.

"Does that feel good, baby girl?" I breathed against her mouth. She made a little noise that I figured meant yes as her mouth dropped open and her eyes closed. "Tell me. Use your words, Quinlan."

"God, you feel so good," she breathed as her hips kept moving in little figure eights. She swore and started moving a little faster, rolling and squeezing herself on my dick in the most delicious way.

"You're so wet, princess. Is this what turns you on?" She nodded, moving a little faster. "Does it turn you on to know I broke his ribs? I kicked him so hard I felt his ribs crack." She moaned and wrapped her arms tighter around my neck. "I straddled him and punched him for daring to look at you. For having the audacity to touch what is mine."

"Please, Jack," she said, burying her face in my neck.

"Say it again."

"Please," she whined.

"God, you sound pathetic. My sweet little slut. Mine to use how I see fit," I growled as my fingertips dug painfully into her flesh. She groaned and pushed harder down onto me.

"No one touches what's mine, Quinlan. Do you hear me?" I reared back and slapped her ass hard, enough I knew it would leave a handprint. She cried out and began lifting herself up and down, impaling herself on me over and over again. "You will never let anyone else," I said, landing another smack on her ass. "Touch you." Smack. "Ever." Smack. "Again." Smack.

She screamed my name and fell down on me one last time, squeezing me for all she was worth.

Don't come. Don't come. Don't come, I repeated over and over again in my head. I did not want it to end yet. I was going to savor this. I never wanted to be anywhere else but here ever again. Me inside of her. Her screaming my name. It was my own slice of heaven.

While she rode the wave of her orgasm, I gathered some of her cream on the tip of my finger, bringing it back to an even tighter hole I had yet to explore that night. Her breath hitched as I circled it, bringing more and more of her release back onto it.

"Have you ever had anything in here?" I asked, kissing the sweat off her neck.

"No," she said, still panting.

"Relax," I said as I pushed the very tip of my finger in slowly. Once I was up to the first knuckle, she started making the most adorable little whimpering noises. Her hips started to move again. Her breath picked up into little excited pants. I pushed in to another knuckle.

"Oh my God, Jack," she moaned into my ear. I started moving it slowly in and out of her ass, moving her hips in the same rhythm. Each time, I went a little deeper until my entire finger was sheathed inside of her.

"Come on, baby girl," I urged her. With my finger moving inside of her, my cock filling her up, and her clit grinding against my body, I knew it wouldn't take her long to come again.

"Holy shit," she whispered as I felt her climax again, her greedy little cunt trying to squeeze my dick clean off.

"Quinlan, shit. You're so tight. I don't think I'm going to last much longer like this." I slowly pulled my finger out of her as she came down and regained control of her breathing. "I want to fuck you now," I murmured in her ear. "I want to mark you as mine with my own release."

She lifted her head, and I pushed her hair, damp with sweat, off her brow. Her eye makeup was smeared across her face, and her lips were swollen.

"Do it, then," she said in that bratty voice of hers that I loved so much. I smiled and stood up, causing her to fall off my lap and onto the floor. I looked down at her, my dick pointing directly at her face.

"Asshole," she said, moving to her hands and knees to stand up.

"Not tonight, babe. We have to work you up to that." She looked up at me with a scowl. I moved to her side and reached down, wrapping my arm around her middle and lifting her up. She yelped and caught herself with her hands on the couch before she face-planted. I pushed the fabric of her dress up and out of the way.

Before she could open that mouth again, I gripped both sides of her hips and slammed home. I squeezed her ass where I had left the sexiest handprints and used my thumbs to spread her cheeks. I wanted a good view of both holes as I fucked her senseless. I slid out slowly and then back in, watching her stretch for me. She was so wet, so pink, so pretty.

I began to move in rhythmic strokes, bottoming out inside of her each time and watching her struggle to remain standing. I snaked one of my hands around her hips and found her clit, gently massaging the little nub. I was rewarded with the sweet sound of her moaning.

She swore as I picked up the pace, crashing into her like a man possessed.

"Yes, yes, yes," she repeated over and over again.

"Remember," I said down to her. "When you come around my cock again, I want everyone in this building to hear you. I want every single one of them to know you are mine, do you understand?"

And then the next words that came out of her mouth pushed me over the edge and had my head spinning.

"Yes, Daddy," she whimpered. "Please, make me come." My hips stuttered, and I pinched her swollen nub, making her cry out. A wave of heat flooded my veins, and I felt myself spill into her with her name on my lips. I was barely able to register that she had screamed my name as well before letting her face fall into the cushions.

She twitched around me, milking me for every last drop I was able to give. I held her up by her hips as I slid out of her.

"Are you on the pill?" I asked, completely out of breath.

She nodded.

"Good," I answered. "Because I want you to keep me inside of you until I'm put back together and ready to go." I smacked her ass again. "Keep these hips up, and don't spill a drop."

14

I tucked myself back into my boxers and pulled my jeans back on before I straightened my shirt and walked around to my desk to pick up a few files I was going to need over the next few days. I looked over at her, still standing there completely bared to me.

Her face was pressed into the cushions of the couch, and her ass was up as high as she could get it. So high I saw her legs begin to shake with the effort. It probably didn't help that she had a sore ankle, but this was part of her punishment for letting that man touch her and see her.

She whined and shifted her feet, making her hips sway back and forth. I walked back over to her and watched my cum slowly leak out of her as her legs started to give out.

"I don't think I've ever seen anything so sexy in my life," I said. "But I wasn't ready to go yet." She whimpered, and I smacked her bare pussy just as hard as I had smacked her ass earlier.

She cried out, and her legs gave way. Falling down onto the floor, she looked up at me with a pout.

"Bad girl," I scolded. "Get up." My voice was hard and demanding, causing her to scurry to her feet. She rubbed her thighs together, no doubt feeling my release flowing freely out of her and coating her thighs. She leaned to one side, clearly favoring her right ankle.

"I'm sorry," she said. "My ankle just hurts."

"What else are you sorry for, Quinlan?"

Her eyebrows drew together, and her voice shook when she answered. "I'm sorry. I don't know what you mean."

"Are you sorry that you let another man touch you?" I asked, taking a step toward her. "Are you sorry you let another man lay his eyes on my sweet little pussy?"

"Yes, sir," she said.

"Say it," I said, wrapping my hand around her jaw and looking into her wide eyes.

"I'm sorry I let another man touch me. And I'm sorry I let him see me."

"You will sit the entire ride home with my cum between your legs as a reminder of who you belong to tonight." She nodded her head. I leaned down and kissed her.

She opened her mouth to me, soaking up my forgiveness like a sponge. I licked and bit and sucked on her mouth until she had fallen into me, using my body to hold hers up. My hand remained tight on her jaw, but my other arm wrapped around her waist to help support her weight.

I pulled away and looked into her eyes. I saw so much trust in them that it made my stomach flip. I found myself wondering again where the hell she had come from. I kissed her nose and then picked her up like a child, making sure my arm under her thighs was far enough down that it would cover her as we walked out of the club.

"That didn't seem to last too long," Hudson said as we emerged from the hallway.

"Yeah, Jacky boy," Wes agreed. "Have you lost your touch?" They all laughed, and I was about to jump in and tell them all to go to hell, but Quinlan beat me to it.

"Guys," she said in a chastising voice. "Be nice. You wouldn't last two seconds with this grade A coochie either." They all bust out laughing while she sat there looking pleased as punch.

"Thanks for still insinuating I didn't last long enough," I said only to her. She laughed and turned her attention back to the guys.

"It was nice meeting you," she said.

"Come back anytime, Quin," Wes said, grinning from ear to ear.

"Yeah, love," Hudson said. "Maybe next time bring a friend for me, eh?"

"Man whore!" Owen called from the balcony. "See you next time, Quin."

She looked up at him and smiled. "Maybe next time we'll skip the fighting?"

"Where's the fun in that?" Greg chimed in, grinning at us from where he sat at the bar. "Until next time, love."

"See you guys later. Let Anders know that if he needs anything, I'm indisposed until morning."

"You mean afternoon!" Wes called as I pushed through the door.

"The afternoon is my morning!" I called back and let the door shut behind us.

The valet had pulled my car to the front of the club, presumably when the fight had broken out in case I was ready to leave quickly.

"Sorry about keeping you waiting," I said to the two guys standing next to the valet stand.

"No worries, boss."

Quinlan snorted at that, and when I buckled her into the passenger seat, I tugged it tighter than necessary.

"Something funny, Q?" I asked, leaning over her and invading her space in the small sports car.

"Nope!" She popped the *P* sound and smiled up at me. I kissed her dark lips and walked over to tip the valet. I probably looked a wreck at this point with dark lipstick smeared all over my mouth and makeup staining my neck, but I didn't really care. Everyone here had seen far worse from me and the crew inside.

"Get home safe, guys, okay?" I called over my shoulder at them as I rounded my car. They nodded and went back to talking as they closed everything up for the night.

I glanced down at the dashboard.

"Midnight," she sighed, following my gaze. "Do

you know when the last time was that I was awake at midnight?"

I started the car and shifted, taking off back to my house. "When?" I smiled over at her.

"Probably a year at least," she said, leaning her head back on the headrest. "Well, maybe a little less than a year. The last time I went out and stayed out late was for my twenty-third birthday."

"When's your birthday?" I asked.

"Next month. The fourteenth." She yawned. "When's your birthday? Wait, how old are you?"

"I just turned twenty-seven in December. I was a Christmas miracle."

"Hah!" She snorted. "I bet you were. That's just what every woman wants to be doing on Christmas Day—shoving a square peg through a round hole."

I looked over at her, and when we locked eyes for a second, we both just burst out laughing.

"Just saying," she said, coming out of her laughing fit.

"Okay, fair enough," I said. "But look at the absolute angel I turned into. I'm a gift from God himself."

"And humble," she countered.

"Very humble. So tell me more about this author dream of yours."

She adjusted herself in the seat, and my mind wandered back to what had just happened in my office before she broke the silence.

"I always wanted to be a writer," she said as she stared out the window. "I kind of fell into this gig because I needed something to pay the bills while I wrote out all of my stories. It pays well, it's writing, and they have a great healthcare plan," she quipped.

"Okay, so how long have you worked there?"

"About two years? I started working there right after college as an intern and then just kind of worked my way up."

"Why haven't you tried to get your books published?"

She sighed and turned her gaze on me and then down at my hand as it switched gears, getting on the highway back to mine. Her fingertips danced across my hand, and I flipped it over and grabbed them, letting her fingers fit between mine.

"I'm terrified," she confessed. "What if no one likes them? I do not have a thick skin. Reading bad reviews about my book would probably send me into a spiral." She cleared her throat and went on. "One reason I have kind of broken ties with my family is because I had a little bit of a breakdown after high school."

I squeezed her hand.

"I won't judge you," I reassured her. "I've been through plenty of shit myself, Q. I'm the last person that would judge you for this."

She sighed and ran a hand through her hair.

"Yeah, well," she murmured. "The summer after my senior year, I tried to kill myself."

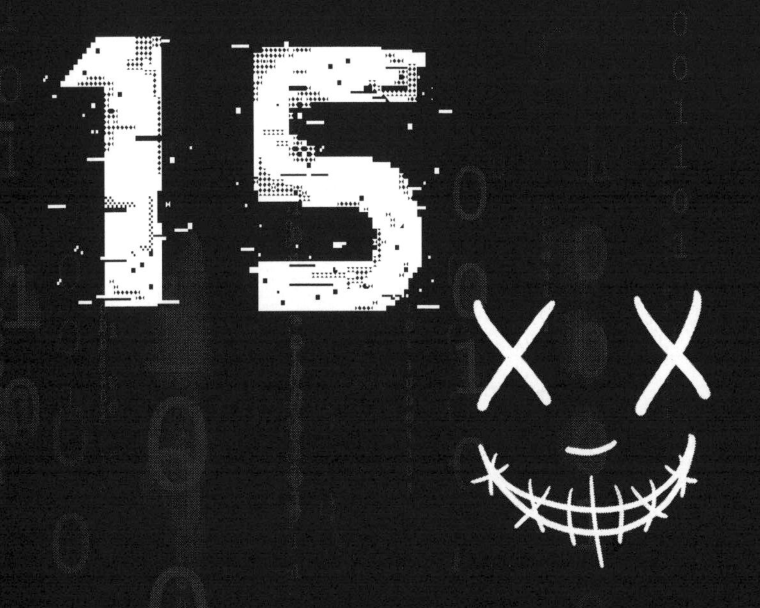

My chest felt like it was going to cave in on itself. The thought of Quinlan killing herself had almost stopped my heart. I squeezed her hand even tighter.

"My family was putting too much pressure on me to be perfect. I was putting too much pressure on myself to be perfect. I had to have perfect grades, a perfect body, and go to the perfect college. I was starving myself, trying to stay in the size twos my mom kept hanging in my closet. I was buying Adderall from the drug dealers at my school and paying them double just to keep them quiet. I needed it to stay up nonstop studying to get into Harvard or Yale.

"And then one day, I was home alone when the mail came. I had a letter from Harvard. Before I even opened it, I had decided that if I didn't get in, I was going to end it. There was no way I could look my parents in the eye and tell them I didn't get into another one of their prestigious schools. Yale had already turned me away, and the look on their faces was just...disgust.

"So I went to the kitchen, our big, white kitchen that had windows that overlooked the ocean, and grabbed a letter opener out of the drawer to the left side of the sink. It was silver and had these hydrangea flowers etched into the handle," she said, looking over at me with a small smile before continuing. "I cut open the letter, pulled it out, and unfolded it.

"'Miss Van Haas,' it started out. 'We regret to inform you that...' But I didn't continue. That was enough. I knew what it was going to tell me. It was going to tell me I wasn't good enough. I wasn't smart enough. I wasn't skinny enough. I wasn't perfect enough. I wasn't anything. I just wasn't enough." She took a breath and wiped furiously at her face.

"So I held that letter opener in my right hand and pointed the tip of it to the inside of my forearm. Down the highway, not across it, I could remember some idiot saying in class one day. I can remember," she said, kind of trailing off, "that it didn't hurt as much as I expected it to."

It was hard for me to breathe just sitting there listening to her tell me all of this. My throat was burning, and I was blinking back my own tears. I had never known anyone that had attempted suicide until now. I wanted nothing more than to pull over on the side of the road and pull her onto my lap, attempting to leach every ounce of pain out of her.

"Anyway," she said softly. "My parents found me there on the kitchen floor a few minutes later. They had come home from playing tennis and stepped in the puddle of blood that had started to seep into the rug under the sink. I was taken to the hospital, and I guess the rest is history. I was institutionalized for the rest of the school term and through the summer. I missed graduation, but I was honestly thankful for it. Nothing would've been worse than standing in front of my family and friends after that."

"Quinlan," I said softly and stroked her hand with my thumb. "I'm so sorry."

"I got the help I needed," she said, turning her head to look at me. I used my left hand to quickly shift down as we exited the highway and entered the suburbs where I lived. "I went through a lot of therapy and got on the right meds to help me through it. I still go to therapy once a week, and I'm on a delightful cocktail of medication to get me through the day." She laughed softly.

"I'm so much better out here," she said as we pulled into my driveway. "You can't understand how suffocating it is living that kind of life until you get out of it. California is so open and sunny and just happy all the time. California is all yellows, oranges, and reds. New England was just grey and blues. The colors are brighter here. The wind is warmer."

I turned toward her after I had parked and wiped the remaining tears off her cheeks. "Thank you for sharing that with me."

She smiled and nodded. "You've shared a lot with me tonight. I wanted you to have a piece of me to keep when I leave in the morning. Is that silly?"

I had thought her beautiful before. But with the vulnerability I saw in her eyes when she asked me that question? Breathtaking. Nothing, not even her face when she laughed with my friends or her chubby cheeks when she stuffed her mouth full of pizza or even her moans when she was writhing underneath me, could compare to how she looked in that moment.

I stared at her for a moment, drinking her in.

Tell her you want it to be more than a night. Nut up and tell her you want to see her again. Stop being a fucking coward.

"It's not silly, Quinlan," I finally answered.

She smiled and turned to open the door, but I grabbed her arm and pulled her back to me. I could taste the salty tears on her lips as I ran my tongue over them. She opened her mouth to me, and I invaded hers. I was softer with her than I had been before. I wanted this kiss to communicate something to her I was too afraid to say out loud.

"I really, really need a shower," she said, breaking the kiss. She gave me another quick peck and then climbed out of the car. I laid my head back, running my hands through my hair, and sighed.

"What the fuck are you doing, Jack," I muttered to myself before following her inside.

She was sleeping. I had slipped into the shower with her and washed her hair. Her face lit up with laughter when I washed her body and couldn't stop soaping up her boobs. She rinsed off, and I made sure all of her makeup was off her face for her. I had kissed her mouth, her jaw, her neck, her chest, and down her stomach, nibbling on her hips.

She had leaned back against the shower wall while I gave her her eighth orgasm of the night.

But who was counting.

I gave her one of my hoodies to put on even though she had protested, saying she would be too big for it to fit properly. I hated the little pieces of self-hatred she carried over from years ago. I had pulled the hoodie over her head and watched it engulf her, damn near swallowing her whole. It was just long enough to cover her ass, and I loved how it peeked out every time she lifted her arms to push her hair off her shoulders.

While she got ready for bed, I put fresh sheets on the bed and rolled them down for her. She ran and jumped into them and sighed, rubbing her legs and feet on the soft fabric.

And then she fell asleep, relaxed in my arms and on my chest, one leg thrown over mine. She was hanging on to me like a koala. I had planned for this night to last so much longer than it had. As I lay there, listening to her breathing and her phone playing white noise (she supposedly couldn't sleep without a fan, and I had not a single one in the entire house), I wished I could make time slow down for the next few hours.

And not just because I wanted more of this, the sweet moments where she was quiet and calm. No, I wanted more time because I had so many more things I wanted to do to her body. Yes, I wanted more of her laughter, and I wanted her to share more pieces of herself with me. But I also wanted to hear her begging for it. I wanted to see how many other ways I could make her body hum for me.

This was a one-night-only thing, I told myself over and over again. *You aren't supposed to be letting her sleep the night away. You're supposed to bring out all your toys and watch her break for you.*

But there we were, lying in bed together, her sleeping and me pondering what the hell I had gotten myself into. I could have easily kept her up the rest of the night. I never went to sleep before the sun came up anyway. I was always streaming, working on shit for the clubs, or just watching TV.

Insomnia at its finest.

But she was tired. I had seen her eyes drooping on the way home, and she could barely hold herself up after she was done with her shower. It took her all of five minutes to fall asleep next to me. And because of that, I couldn't keep her up. I didn't actually *want* to keep her up if I was completely honest with myself.

My dick had fought me hard on that subject, but my sensible side had won over. Going into the type of rough play I wanted to partake in with her tired, raw, and probably still very emotional from the conversation in the car wouldn't have been fair. She wouldn't have been in the right headspace to enjoy it.

What she needed was rest and care.

I carefully reached over to the bedside table and grabbed my phone. I turned the brightness all the way down and checked my texts. Of course, each one of them had texted me since we left the club. They were worse than old women, constantly having their noses in everyone's business but their own.

Wes: I swear to fucking god man if you let her walk out of your house in the morning for good I will never forgive you. I love her. Not to be dramatic, but I would die for Quin.

I snorted. *Idiot.*

Owen: Everything has been taken care of thanks to my quick thinking and very resourceful family. Tell Quin I say hello and that if she gets tired of your stupid games, my door is always open.

My eye twitched at that one. Little shit knew exactly what to say to push my buttons.

Hudson: You better have taken my advice because if I never see her again I'm going to be heartbroken. Wes and I are in love.

Greg: I imagine I agree with whatever everyone else is typing and sending to you right now. Don't be a dick. We just want to see you happy, man. She matches your energy. And if she can put up with your shit, you better keep her.

I created a group chat with all four of them.

I'll tell her.

Send.

Now fuck off. She's sleeping.

My phone vibrated a few more times before I was able to sit it back on the stand, but I didn't care. I would check it in the morning. And I already knew what they were saying.

I yawned and pulled the covers higher. Maybe I would be able to sleep after all. I closed my eyes and counted Quinlan's breaths until sleep found me.

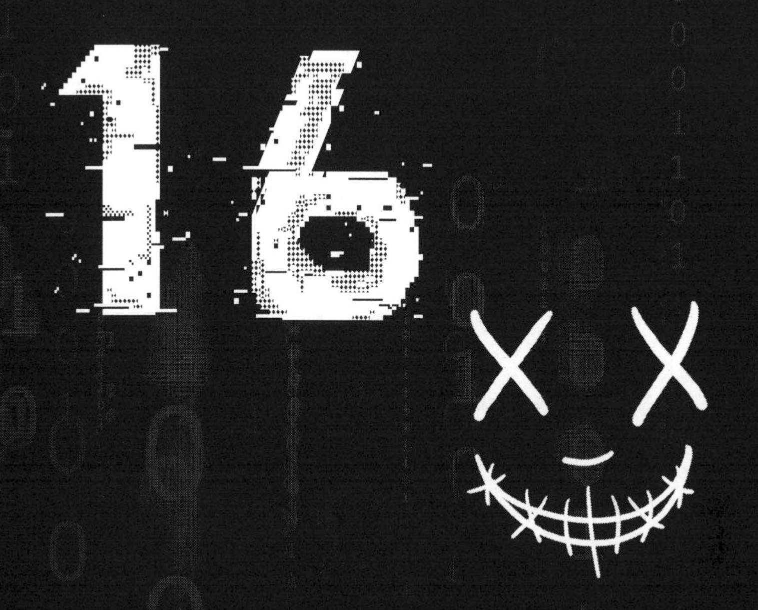

16

I didn't know who woke up first, but suddenly she was facing me, and her leg was in the crook of my arm, opening her wide. Then I was inside of her, moving and stroking her slowly. Our foreheads fell together, and our noses touched. Our breaths mixed together as our lips hovered over each other's, just close enough to barely touch.

She was so wet and warm. I ground into her as deep as I could, angling her so that her clit could move against my pelvis. My free hand tangled in her hair, anchoring her to me as I picked up speed.

"You feel so good," she whispered. "I never thought I would have this," she admitted. I hit a certain spot inside of her that had her whimpering.

"Have what?" I asked, panting and trying to hold back from just pounding her into the mattress.

"Someone that could make me feel like this." She moaned and started meeting my thrusts as much as she could in the position I had her. "It's going to be very hard to go back to pretending after this," she said with a breathy little laugh.

A wave of irrational jealousy crashed through me, and I kissed her to keep her from saying anything else that was going to set me off. In a very caveman-like gesture, I flipped her onto her back and put both of her legs on my shoulders, taking control.

When I slid back into her wet heat, I felt her shiver against me. I leaned forward and started rutting against her like a man possessed. My thumb found her clit, and she immediately cried out, her walls clutching me like a lifeline. I fell over the edge a moment later, claiming her for myself and ruining her for any other man or woman that might cross her path.

"You don't have to," I finally said as the last of my seed spilled into her. Her legs dropped from my shoulders and fell around my hips. She ground against me, still needy, and fuck did she look hot doing it. My fingertips gently started to move between her folds, moving around that little bundle of nerves but not quite touching it.

"Don't have to what?" she asked, moving faster against me.

"Fuck," I whispered as she continued to move against my softening cock, the friction making my abs jump. "You don't have to go back to pretending," I ground out.

Her head pressed back into the pillows as she took what she needed from me, coming again on my cock. I felt her coat me with liquid heat as I twitched inside of her, struggling not to move. I was overstimulated in the best way.

I groaned and watched her chest rise and fall as she came down. She moved to let me free, but I grabbed her hips and held her against me. I could feel both of our releases leaking out between where we were joined, and it was almost hot enough to get me going again.

"You don't have to go back to pretending." Her pussy moved against me again, and I jerked a little, the stimulation sending an electric shock to my stomach. "We could extend this little game."

She smiled up at me in the darkness. "You want me for another night, Joker?" she asked, licking her lips.

"Or longer," I hedged, wondering if she was going to turn me down. I hadn't really thought it through. I shouldn't have asked her while I was still inside of her. I cringed at how manipulating that could seem. I hadn't meant to. It had just come out of my mouth like fucking word vomit.

She was silent a moment too long.

"I— Sorry. I'll go get a cloth, hold on," I said lamely and eased out of her, making my way to the bathroom and not looking at her.

"Fucking idiot," I whispered to myself when I turned on the water. As I waited for it to warm up, I stared at myself in the mirror. "This is why you don't do relationships anymore," I said, pointing an accusing finger at myself.

I wet the washcloth with warm water and cleaned myself off before sticking it back under the water and rinsing it out for her. I hated being caught off guard. I was going to have to fight through the embarrassment and just go back in there and apologize.

I was walking myself through how I was going to do that while I let the hot water flow over my fingers. And then her warm hands were at my back and circling themselves around my waist. She planted a kiss in between my shoulder blades as I waited.

"You bolted out of there pretty quickly," she murmured into my back. "Were you asking me out?"

I turned the faucet off and turned around in her arms. I let my wet hands rest on the counter behind me while she kept her arms wrapped firmly around my waist. I was starting to feel smothered by the possibility of her saying no.

"Yes," I answered.

"It took you long enough," she said with a smile. "I mean, I honestly thought that you would ask me after Hudson gave you so much shit for it in the hallway."

"Oh, you heard that, did you?" I asked, breathing a sigh of relief. "Eavesdropping, naughty girl?"

"You can punish me for it later," she said, staring up at me with a challenge in those coffee-colored eyes.

"Is that a yes, Curly Q?" I wrapped a strand of her wavy hair around my fingers. It had air-dried after our shower earlier with the softest curls.

"I guess," she said with a shrug and a smile. I grinned down at her and then bent over and threw her over my shoulder before she could protest. She squealed and gripped my waist.

"Such a brat." Picking up the clean cloth from the counter with my free hand, I cleaned her up as best I could, watching the reflection of us in the mirror. "You're so fucking perfect, you know that?" I asked, dropping the dirty cloth back to the counter.

I spread her open with my fingers, taking in the beautiful sight of her swollen and sore from our night together. Her breaths picked up a bit as I explored with my fingers, watching her become wet all over again. She was so fucking responsive. I dipped a finger inside of her, and she gasped against me.

"Too bad brats don't deserve orgasms," I said, pulling my finger out of her and landing a hard smack on her pussy before carrying her back to the bed.

"Please, Jack," she whined, trying to rub her thighs together. "You started it!"

"You're going to lie here and sleep the rest of the night. If you behave, I'll reward you in the morning. Stop," I commanded, gripping one of her thighs that wouldn't stop moving, searching for any relief. My little pet was insatiable, and I fucking loved it.

"Please," she tried again.

"No. Go to sleep. And don't you dare touch yourself, or I will spank you so hard before you leave for work in the morning that you won't be able to sit down. Got it?"

She groaned and sighed. "Fine, I'll behave," she huffed. "I'm fucking exhausted anyway," she said and then, as if proving her point, yawned dramatically.

"Go to sleep and stop trying to use me for orgasms, then."

"If you insist," she mumbled, already half-asleep, and went silent.

I stroked her hair and breathed in her scent as she relaxed and fell back asleep. Once she was finally asleep, I was finally able to let myself smile broadly, excited at the prospect of dating this wild little thing in my arms. The guys were going to give me so much shit for them being right. I rolled my eyes thinking about it.

When the sun started to come up, my mind finally exhausted itself and let me drift back to sleep.

I woke up and blinked against the bright sunlight streaming through my blinds. I rolled onto my side and checked the time on my phone. It was already noon.

"Shit," I swore and rolled over to wake Quinlan up. "Q, you are so, so late," I said as I rolled all the way over to find myself alone in bed.

The fuck?

I threw the covers off and stalked through the house, saying her name and looking for any sign of her. All of her clothes and work shit was gone. I peered out of the window, and her car was gone. I ran my hands through my hair, a sinking feeling filling up my gut.

Had she just decided to leave?

And then a real panic sank in.

Had she played me? Did she just fuck around and go along with everything just to expose me and catch some big break at work?

"No, Jack," I said out loud to myself. "She signed NDAs."

But she had really only signed anything that prohibited her from telling anyone my real name. She could easily get around those by talking about our night together and all the things we did.

"Shut up," I muttered, walking back into my room. "She may have left a note."

I sighed when I made my way over to the side she had slept on and found a small slip of paper on the floor that must've fallen off sometime after she left.

I called myself pathetic and bent over to pick it up.

I have to work until 5.
Text me when you wake up, Joker.
524-333-1167
-Q

Just over five hours until she was back in my space, filling it up with her laughter and sass mouth. I hadn't had something, some*one*, to look forward to in so long I wasn't sure what to do with myself.

I took the note she had written me and stuffed it in the bottom of my sock drawer. I didn't know what possessed me to keep it, but in that moment, I couldn't throw it away. I covered it up and closed the drawer.

Glancing over at the bed, still rumpled on *both* sides, I smiled to myself.

Five hours.

EPILOGUE

A YEAR LATER

I watched her as we sat outside, the setting sun catching her hair on fire as she sipped her wine. Her head fell back on the chair, and she closed her eyes. My stomach was in knots with anxiety as I tried to remember everything I wanted to say to her.

I had convinced her to move in with me about six months ago because she was spending more time here, and her poor plants were suffering. The house had gone from looking like a show house to looking like a lived-in home pretty quickly. Every day I swore I found a new plant hanging from the ceiling or shoved on a shelf near a window.

Instead of going to sleep alone every night, I

now had her to look forward to after I finished streaming. I could sneak in and take her in my arms, my hand snaking between her thighs as she sighed and moved against me.

Looking at her in the skimpy bathing suit she was wearing, even though the nights had almost gotten too cool for swimming, my eyes caught on the little bite marks and fingertip bruises painted on her skin. It was her favorite thing for me to do, mark her in some way almost every night so that she could look at them as a reminder each morning.

"Hey," I said, holding my arm out toward her. She grabbed my hand, sitting her wine on the table, and came to sit on my lap. "You know I love you, right?"

"Yes," she said hesitantly.

"You are everything to me, Quinlan. You found me when I had honestly given up on ever finding anyone. I was alone, hiding, and shut off to anyone, and in you walked with your big eyes and sass mouth and swept me right off my feet. You gave me something I didn't know I could have."

She laughed and leaned in for a kiss. Her mouth tasted like sunshine and wine.

"My sass mouth is my best feature, I've been told," she said, smiling at me.

"I beg to differ. Anyone that says that hasn't seen your ass." To make my point, I squeezed it, and she gave a little yelp. It was probably still sore from the beating it took last night.

"You're not too shabby yourself," she said with a smirk. "I've decided I'll keep you around."

"Good to know," I said, pulling her closer against my chest. "Because I was wondering if you'd like to play another game?"

"What kind of game?" She sat up straighter and looked at me with suspicion.

"So," I said, fishing in my pocket and trying to hold her at the same time. "It's kind of a similar game to our first one."

"The 'for one night only, let's have fun' one?" she asked, her eyebrow raised.

"Yeah, but instead of it being just one night," I said as my fingers finally found the hard stone in my pocket, "I was wondering if you'd like to make it a little more permanent?" I pulled the ring out of my pocket and held it up for her to see.

Her mouth dropped open, and her eyes went wide, shifting from the ring to me and back again. I grinned.

"I—what?" she stuttered.

"Will you marry me, Curly Q?"

Something between a laugh and a cry burst out of her as she threw her arms around my neck, practically cutting off my airway. She hiccoughed and threaded her fingers through my hair. A few of her deep breaths later and I was starting to get worried I wasn't going to get an answer. My arm that was around her waist squeezed.

"So," I said, her arms muffling my voice. "Is that a yes or…?"

She pushed back and grabbed my face in both of her hands, staring straight into my fucking soul. I would never get used to how she could take my breath away with a single look.

"Yes," she said and then shoved her left hand in between us, signaling for me to slip the ring on her finger. It was a salt-and-pepper emerald-cut diamond surrounded by a halo of baguette-cut white diamonds.

Had I known what any of that meant before I picked it out? No. But I asked around her friends, paid attention to her Pinterest boards, and ignored every single piece of advice any of my friends had to give.

It went on and fit snugly against her finger. Warmth spread through my body seeing a physical representation of my claim on her. I looked up at her, watching the tears fall over her cheeks as she wiped at them viciously. She was so pretty when she cried.

"It's beautiful. I love it." She kissed me, and I licked the salty tears off her lips. "I love you." She kissed me again.

As the kiss deepened, my cock took the hint and came to life, growing hard underneath her. She moaned into my mouth as she shifted her weight, trying to straddle across my hips.

"I will never get sick of this," she said against my mouth. My hands roamed across her body, squeezing and groping every ounce of flesh I could get. "Wanna fuck your fiancée?" she asked as she began to climb off my lap. Her smile was a challenge that I was ready to accept.

Her hands went behind her back, untying the strands of her bikini top. It fell to the ground at her feet, and my cock strained almost painfully against my jeans. I leaned back in the chair and adjusted myself. Her eyes went to my crotch, and she licked her lips.

"And the bottoms," I said, motioning to the little piece of fabric barely covering her lower half. Her eyes met mine again, and her lips curved up in a seductive smile. Slowly, so fucking slowly, she turned around to give me the full view of her sex as she pulled them off her ass and down those toned thighs. I drank in every second of it. She stood back up, stepping out of them and turning back around to face me.

She looked at me expectantly, waiting for my command like the good little girl she was. I made her stand there for a while, letting her grow frustrated and flushed under my gaze before taking control.

"Get on your knees."

She smirked, her eyes turning ornery, and then suddenly she took off, laughing and running back into the house. My blood heated, and my dick twitched at the challenge.

Game on.

Follow Wes' story in the next book in the One Night series, Secrets We Hunt here: Secrets We Hunt

ACKNOWLEDGMENTS

First to the reader, thank you for taking a chance on my faceless gamer fantasy. For anyone who loves the likes of Corpse, Skypso, vo.Eros and the like, this one was for you.

Abi, thank you for bringing my cover to life. It was everything I dreamed of for this book and more.

Sandra, thank you for the little notes you leave me in my edits to let me know how hot the scenes are. They always make me laugh. And thank you for going in blind to every story. It cracks me up to think of you going into this one without a clue as to what it was about.

Eros, thank you for putting up with all of my questions, constant messages about this book, and for doing the audiobook. You have no idea how much it means to me for you to bring this character to life.

A.D. McCammon, B.L. Mute, Liza James, and C.E. Ricci, thank you for having your messages constantly open to me whether it be for advice or just to listen to me obsess over you and your words. Seriously. I love you all. I aspire to be as cool as each one of you one day.

Tasha, babe, thank you for supporting me always. Thank you for being a beta reader for these two and giving me feedback. I always wanted to be an author you recommended so when you read and loved my work, it meant so, so much to me. Love you forever, Smutty Slut.

Arianna, Brittany, Bea, Hadeel, Hannah, Jacky, Jordan, Lauren, Mika, Niki, and Stevie, thank you for your constant pushing to get me where I am. You always take the time to read scenes or let me bounce ideas off of all of you and I am forever grateful. Thank you for always being thirsty enough to read my smut.

ABOUT THE AUTHOR

Dana Isaly is a writer of dark romance, fantasy romance, and has also been known to dabble in poetry (it was a phase in college, leave her alone).

She was born in the Midwest and has been all over but now resides (begrudgingly) in Alabama. She is a lover of books, coffee, and rainy days. Dana is probably the only person in the writing community that is actually a morning person.

She swears too much, is way too comfortable on her TikTok, and believes that love is love is love.

You can find her on Instagram (@danaisalyauthorpage) or on Facebook with the same name. Honestly though, the best place to get in touch with her is on TikTok (@authordanaisaly) because she isn't great with any other social media.

Sign up for my newsletter here:
http://eepurl.com/hDrCGb

ALSO BY DANA ISALY

The Triad Series

Scars (The Triad Series Book 1)

Liars (The Triad Series Book 2)

The Esteria Series

Flame and Starlight

Flame and Starlight 2

Games We Play

Standalone

Obsession